MW01193789

Bug Hollow

ALSO BY MICHELLE HUNEVEN

Search

Off Course

Blame

Jamesland

Round Rock

Bug Hollow

A NOVEL

Michelle Huneven

PENGUIN PRESS NEW YORK 2025

PENGUIN PRESS
An imprint of Penguin Random House LLC
1745 Broadway, New York, NY 10019
penguinrandomhouse.com

Portions of this book originally appeared in a different form in *StoryQuarterly*, issue 55.

Designed by Alexis Farabaugh

LIBRARY OF CONGRESS CATALOGING-IN-PUBLICATION DATA

Names: Huneven, Michelle, 1953– author
Title: Bug Hollow : a novel / Michelle Huneven.
Description: New York : Penguin Press, 2025. |
Identifiers: LCCN 2025000450 (print) |
LCCN 2025000451 (ebook) | ISBN 9780593834879 hardcover |
ISBN 9780593834886 ebook
Subjects: LCGFT: Domestic fiction
Classification: LCC PS3558.U4662 B84 2025 (print) |
LCC PS3558.U4662 (ebook) | DDC 813/.54—dc23/eng/20250206
LC record available at https://lccn.loc.gov/2025000450
LC ebook record available at https://lccn.loc.gov/2025000451

Printed in the United States of America
1st Printing

The authorized representative in the EU for product safety and compliance is Penguin Random House Ireland, Morrison Chambers, 32 Nassau Street, Dublin D02 YH68, Ireland, https://eu-contact.penguin.ie.

To Altadena

Contents

Bug Hollow

Bug Hollow

The summer when Sally Samuelson was eight, her brother Ellis graduated from high school and a few days later, he and his best friends, Heck Stevens and Ben Klosterman, drove up the coast in Heck's '64 Rambler American. They promised to be back in a week. Sally was the only one who went outside to see them off. She waved a dishrag and dabbed at pretend tears, then one or two real ones. "Bye, little Pips!" Ellis yelled from the back seat—he called her Pipsqueak, with variations. "See you in the funny papers!"

Ellis had thick, curly yellow hair long enough to tuck behind his ears and he wore a baseball cap to keep it there. He'd lately grown incredibly tall and skinny; his pants rode so low on his hip bones, they seemed about to slip off. Sally's sister, Katie, who was fourteen, called him El Greck after they saw El Greco's *Christ on the Cross* at the Getty; even their parents confirmed the resemblance.

His last two years in high school, Ellis had a girlfriend named Carla, who was also tall and blond and liked to show off her stomach. In front of Ellis, she would say hi to Sally. Sometimes Ellis would come into Sally's room when she was drawing on the floor; he'd sit by her and talk about his last baseball game or his weird calculus teacher, and sometimes he'd wonder how much he liked Carla and if she was even nice. Sally somehow knew not to say what she thought. Anyway, Ellis spent most of his time playing ball with Ben and Heck. For their trip, they packed Heck's old Rambler with sleeping bags, the small smelly tent the Samuelson kids used on camping trips, and a cooler full of sodas. After ten days, when Ellis hadn't come back, Heck showed up at the Samuelsons' front door with the tent. Sally answered his knock.

"Ellis decided to stay away for a few more days," he said.

"Stay where?" Sally's mother said from behind her.

"With some girl he met," said Heck. "Not sure where, exactly."

"Well, where did they meet?"

"On a beach around Santa Cruz."

That was all her mother could get out of Heck. "Some girl has snagged Ellis," she told Sally's father when he came home from work.

"Good for her," he said.

"How can you say that, Phil?" her mother cried. "El's such an innocent. What if she's trouble?"

Hinky, their Manchester terrier, cocked her head at one parent, then the other; she followed conversations—they'd tested her by standing in a circle and tossing the conversation back and forth. Hinky shifted her attention to each speaker in turn.

"What if he doesn't come back in time for his job?"

Ellis was supposed to be a counselor at the day camp he'd attended since first grade.

"Let's worry about that when the time comes," Sally's father said.

The camp's start date came and went. Carla showed up one night after dinner and wept noisily on their sofa. She also hadn't heard from Ellis. "He was supposed to come with me to my cousin's wedding," she wailed.

"I knew we shouldn't have let him go off like that," Sally's mother said after Carla left. "One fast girl on a beach and he's a goner!"

"I'm sure he's fine," Sally's father said. "It's high time he gave us something to worry about."

Ellis was a straight-A student and a star pitcher, and had a perfect score on the math SAT. He always set the table, and never shut his door, even when Carla or his friends were over. Alone, he listened to sports or studied. He loved baseball above everything and turned down Cal and the University of Chicago when UC San Diego and Ole Miss offered him full baseball scholarships. Their parents regarded the South with what Ellis had called "irrational liberal loathing" and tried to talk him into San Diego. He chose Mississippi.

"What if this girl's a Moonie?" Sally's mother said. "What if he can't get home? He only had seventy dollars."

Hinky looked from one parent to the other.

"Hell, I was younger than he is with only a quarter to my name and I hopped freights all across the country," her father said.

"Oh for god's sake, Phil. Don't start," her mother said.

At sixteen, Sally's father had ridden boxcars from Denver to Boston. He told stories of his hobo days so often that her mother now refused to hear them.

A postcard came showing Monterey Bay.

> *Dear Mom and Dad, Katie, Peeps, and Hinky,*
>
> *Hope you're all well. I'm doing great! I've decided to spend the summer up here. I have a wonderful place to stay and a job. I'll call soon.*
>
> *Love, E.*

Every time the phone rang, everyone froze, then Sally's parents raced to the extensions, with Hinky leaping and barking. *Answer! Get the phone! It might be him!*

The family was supposed to go car camping on the Oregon coast, but now they couldn't, in case Ellis called.

Sally's father went to work in a suit; he was a project manager at Parsons Engineering. Sometimes, he went to Argentina or Saudi Arabia for a few weeks, but he'd put off his next trip till they knew more about Ellis. Her mother taught fourth grade and had the summer off. She lay out on a chaise in shorts and a halter top getting very tan, reading mystery novels, and drinking Hawaiian Punch from a green plastic tumbler. When it got too hot, she moved inside to her bedroom. Sally would peek in at her. "Stop lurking, Sally," she'd say.

Katie stayed in her room and read books except when she practiced piano or went over to her friend Christine's house.

Sally drew pictures in her room or went to play under a row of shaggy eucalyptus trees on the corner of their block. She and a neighborhood girl had built a village of tiny bark huts with a network of tunnels below, digging until their gritty fingers tangled underground. Because the neighbor girl was older, she no longer came as much, so alone, Sally maintained the village, which was often scattered. At dusk, when someone bawled her name, she'd go home.

Her mother was at the grocery store when Ellis phoned. Katie was practicing scales on the piano, and Socorro, their housekeeper, was vacuuming. Belly-flopped and coloring on her bedroom floor, Sally was the only person who heard the phone ring. She answered the hall extension.

"Is that you, Pips? How you doing?"

"It's Ellis!" she screamed down the hall. "ELLL-ISSSS!" Then, into the phone, "Are you coming home?"

"Not yet. But tell me, Pips. How mad are Mom and Dad?"

"Pretty mad."

"Is Mom there?" Ellis asked.

"She's at the store. Hold on." She yelled, "Katie!" at the top of her voice. "She can't hear me," she told Ellis.

"That's okay, Pips. Just tell me, what do Mom and Dad say about me?"

Sally sat on the floor. Hinky planted herself in front of her. Being the one to talk to Ellis felt too important. "Mom thinks you've been kidnapped, and Dad thinks you're having fun." She tried to ESP with Katie—*Come here now!*—but Katie's fingers kept cantering up and down the keys. Sally thought of running to get her, but what if Ellis hung up? Her parents hadn't said what to do if he called when they weren't there. "They really want you to come home, El," she said.

"I can't. I have great job. Guess what it is, Peeps. I work in an ice cream shop."

"Oh." She touched Hinky's curved black toenails.

"And the place I live? There's a swimming hole just out the back door. But real quick, Peeps. How're you and Katie? And Hinky?"

"Hinky's right here," Sally said. "Say hi." She held the receiver to Hinky's ear until her little black brow wrinkled. "Just come home, El," Sally said into the mouthpiece. "Mom's getting mean. And we can't go camping. . . ."

A clatter of tumbling coins and an operator's canned voice said, *Three minutes*. "Got to go," Ellis said. "Tell Mom and Dad not to worry. I love you, Pips."

Love? When had Ellis ever said he loved her or anyone? (Maybe he'd said it to Carla but Sally never heard.) In their family they never said I love you to each other. If Sally kissed or hugged her mother, she would draw back and say, "What brought this on?" Sally smoothed Hinky's ears back and kissed the two tan dots of her eyebrows. When the front door whined open and she heard the rustle of grocery bags, Sally ran into the kitchen. "He called! He called!"

Her mother sat on a kitchen barstool still holding a bag in her arms. Hinky leapt around her. "Is he all right? What did he say? Did you get his number?" she said.

"He works in an ice cream store," Sally panted. "He says don't worry."

"So where is he?" her mother said, still embracing the sack. "Did you find out?"

Katie came into the kitchen. "What's up?"

"Is he coming home? What about college? Did you ask him *anything*?"

Sally stood there.

"Goddamn it, Sally. What's wrong with you?" Her mother heaved the sack of groceries off her lap. A muffled crack, and a pale pink liquid leaked through the bag and spread on the kitchen floor.

Katie left the room. Sally began to cry. Hinky leapt on her mother's lap, but she pushed her off. Sally ran out of the house then, and around the corner to the eucalyptus trees. She curled against one shaggy trunk and vowed never to go home. She'd steal towels off the neighbors' clothesline for blankets and live on the pomegranates and guavas growing in the abandoned sanitorium up the street. Sleepy from crying, she pulled a large shard of bark over her face to make it dark. She woke when Hinky pawed her shoulder. Her father lifted the bark off her face. "Come on now, Sally," he said. "Let's go home."

Dear Mom and Dad,

I hope Pips told you that I'm doing great and not to worry. I've decided to spend the summer here in a big house with eight other people. The rent is very cheap. We take turns cooking. I'll make my famous tofu-mushroom burgers for you someday. My job is a lot of fun and my boss already wants me to be manager. I told him no because of Ole Miss—and yes, I am training every day. A girl here has a great arm and catches everything I send her way.

I would say where I am, but you might come and try to take me home. I'm extremely happy here, so please don't worry. I'll be back in time for college.

I think of all of you all the time. Tell the Hink that the dogs here are big galumphing woodsy dogs and not prancy-dancy smartypants like her.

I'll call soon.

Much Love to Everyone,
Ellis

Much Love! Again, Sally had never heard him say that to anybody before.

Katie said he had to be in a cult, because he had to be brainwashed to cook. The Ellis they knew ate Pop-Tarts right out of the box because he was too lazy to toast them.

Their mother said, "Not sure a cult would let him take a job out in public. But something's fishy." Their father said nonsense, that Ellis was separating, which was natural. "He's making his way in the world."

Carla must have gotten a letter too because she came over and cried again.

Ellis's letter had a postmark: Los Altos, CA. Sally's father phoned the sheriff's office there, but they wouldn't look for Ellis—this was in the mid-1970s and there were far too many runaways for law enforcement to take on. A desk sergeant told Sally's father to run a classified ad in the local small-town papers.

> **Missing since June:** Our son, Ellis Samuelson, 17 years old, 6'2", blond hair, brown eyes, athletic, smart, funny, and greatly missed. Reward.

The ad went in six different small-town papers, and now when the phone rang it was even more of a shock. Sally's mother wept to her best friend. "We're on pins and needles here!"

Sally's mother had become a yanker: She yanked the phone when she answered it; she yanked open doors and drawers to rummage madly, then slammed them shut. She yanked Sally into the car, to the table, away from the comics display at the market. Sometimes, she yanked Sally to her and held her, kissing her head and wetting her hair with tears. Blue bruises in the shape of her fingertips dappled Sally's upper arms.

Katie said, "Just stay out of her way."

But Sally couldn't. She had to see where her mother was, and if she was okay. Now, her mother refused to leave the house in case Ellis called, so Sally's father did the shopping, and the fridge filled with new brands of cheese, lunch meat, mayonnaise, juice. The fancier brands.

Two days after Ellis's eighteenth birthday on August 8 this came:

Dear Mom and Dad, Katie, Pips, and Hinky,

I saw your ad in the paper. Please don't do that again. It embarrassed me. I'm eighteen now and can live where I want. I miss you too. Please don't worry about me. And don't try to come get me because I really can't leave till Aug. 25 because

1. I promised my boss I'd stay till then.

2. I am saving money for school and won't hit my goal till then.

3. I am very happy in this house with my friends and the dogs.

4. I am training very well. I now run an eight-minute mile. Flat. Everyone in the house comes out for pitching and batting practice every night.

I'm sorry to worry you and hope you aren't too mad at me, but I am really truly okay and happier than I have ever been.

Please pet Hinks for me. I'll see you soon. I love you all very much!
Ellis

"I don't understand why we just don't drive up there and go to every ice cream store we can find," Sally's mother said at the dinner table.

"I would if I felt he was in danger," her father said. "And he's right: he can live wherever he wants now."

"You just won't lift a finger," her mother said.

The air stilled. Sally studied the tiny beige, tan, and white hexagons in the Formica tabletop until her father said, "Here, Sally, let's finish these tater tots."

A woman phoned at dinnertime. She'd been wrapping china in newspaper and happened to read the missing-persons ad. She was Ellis's neighbor in the woods near Boulder Creek in the Santa Cruz Mountains. Ellis—"a darling boy"—had done some weed whacking for her. She supplied an address—"I have a son myself, so I know," she said—and refused the reward.

Early the next morning, they loaded the VW camper van with duffels and pillows and snacks as if for any weekend jaunt. "What if Ellis won't come home with us?" Sally asked.

"He won't have a choice," her mother said.

"We'll play it by ear," said her father.

They drove up to Northern California on freeways through yellow dried-out hills and sometimes along the crinkled sea. They ate hamburgers in the car, driving, driving in the summer heat with the windows open, which made it too loud to talk. Not that Katie would've talked to her. Katie took the middle seat and read her book the whole time. Sally, in the far back seat, colored on a newsprint pad, but mostly she stared out the window and imagined living in different houses they passed. Or she looked at the backs of the others in the car and thought, *Who are these people, and why aren't they nicer?* For as long as she could remember—from her very first remembered thought—she'd had a sense of coming from somewhere else, a place of kindness and good humor and justice, where people weren't so grouchy and annoyed and quick to anger. She'd learned to keep an eye on her mother to see what was coming, while at the same time she tried not to irritate her. And ever since Katie started junior high, she couldn't stand Sally, so Sally steered clear of her too, mostly. Only Ellis was kind. The best. Her father, when he was home and not working, was also kind and even interested in what Sally did—he liked watching her draw her "cartoons," as he called them. Her mother was hardly ever that nice. She used to be, when Sally was very little and didn't yet bother her so much.

Boulder Creek looked like mountain towns they'd seen on camping trips: a short main street whose wooden buildings had tall fake fronts. Sally spotted a log-sided burger stand called the Kandy Kone that had a big soft-serve ice cream cone on its sign. "Hey," she said, "maybe that's where Ellis works." But nobody listens to the eight-year-old, and then the town was behind them.

"We're looking for a row of mailboxes," her father said, and there they were, a straggling line of them, some with their mouths open, tongues hanging.

They bumped down a narrow gravel road. Bushes brushed the camper's sides. The road ended in the dirt yard of a huge, shingled house the black-brown color of telephone poles. Crumbling concrete steps led to a wide deep porch with several slumping old sofas on it, and sleeping on those sofas were various dogs, very large dogs who, hearing the van, sat up, stretched, then bounded down the steps barking. Five dogs.

Hinky sprang window to window, front seat to back, clambering all over them and barking back.

Hi! Hi! Come out of that car and let's smell you, the big dogs said.

Nobody opened a door. These were big shepherd mixes. One Doberman.

Two young women came out the front door, both in cutoff shorts and peasant blouses. One was tall with long rippling red hair and the other, even taller one had smooth brown hair in a swishy ponytail. They waded through the rambunctious dogs calling, "They're friendly! They don't bite!" The ponytailed young woman came to the driver's side and Sally's father rolled down his window. "We're the Samuelsons. Ellis's parents."

"Ellis is at work," the young woman said. "He'll be home in an hour. I'm Julia. That's Randi. Why don't you come in and wait. I just made some iced tea."

She and Randi held what dogs they could as the family got out of the van. Then it was a smell-for-all, snouts all over everyone as they headed to the house. Randi, at the top of the steps, turned and said, "Welcome to Bug Hollow."

Inside, the hot, dark house smelled like old smoke. Sally knew right away why Ellis liked it here: the front room with its log rafters, fat saggy sofas, and tatty taxidermy looked like their favorite mountain lodge, the one near Yosemite where, after camping for a week, they'd spend a night to take showers and eat a dinner their mother didn't have to cook. The big, bearded, laughing lodge owner served the kids huge slices of blackberry pie à la mode, and gave Hinky her own scoop.

Julia asked if Sally and Katie wanted to cool off in the swimming hole. Their mother came out to see if it was safe. Dammed with rocks and logs, overhung with thick-limbed oaks, the pool was dark and calm. Water spiders rippled its surface. Half a dozen inner tubes had stalled against the opposite bank. "It's only really deep by the boulder there," Julia said.

Sally and Katie could wear their T-shirts and panties, their mother said. "And no swinging from that." She pointed to a thick rope you had to climb the boulder to reach. She left then with Hinky, yanking the leash every time Hinky tried to sniff something.

Sally waded into the cool water. "I bet Julia is Ellis's girlfriend," she said. "She's nicest."

"No way. The other one's so much prettier," Katie said, still on the bank. "This water looks kind of scummy."

Sally could see rippled sand and pebbles on the bottom. "It's clear here," she said.

Katie came in, bit by bit. They hauled sun-heated black tubes over their heads, then drifted and kicked around the swimming hole for a long time and nobody checked on them. "I wonder why Ellis likes it here. It's so hot and that old house smells," Katie said, then gave a little scream.

A man with a yellow beard stood on the path. Who knew how long he'd been there. "Oh my god, it's El Greck," Katie cried and started slogging out of the water.

He gave them both one-armed hugs. "I missed you toads," he said. "What have you been doing all summer?"

Katie said, "Wondering where *you* were, dumbo, and never going anywhere but the backyard in case you might call."

"Jeez, Katie. Thanks for the guilt trip," he said.

"You should feel guilty," she said. "So which one is your girlfriend?"

Ellis, looking around, called softly. "Julia?"

She came up the path and slipped her arms around him.

"I just wanted to say hi to you guys before I get into it with Mom and Dad," he said. "But I better get it over with." He squeezed Julia and turned toward the house. "Cover me, God, I'm going in."

Katie grabbed her shorts and ran after him. Sally walked back to the house with Julia, who answered all her questions: Yes, she was in college, at UC Santa Cruz; she was majoring in art to become an artist. And yes, she was older than Ellis, two years and two months older.

"Wow," said Sally. The boys two years younger than her were just starting first grade, very small and dopey. She couldn't imagine liking any one of them.

"Ellis is very mature for his age," Julia said. "He says that you like to draw. Shall we draw some pictures together?"

They sat at the long wooden dining table with some thick paper and Julia's big box of oil pastels. They could hear the murmur of El and the parents talking above them, on the second floor, but not what they were saying. At Julia's suggestion, they drew squiggles for each other. Of the two long narrow loops Sally gave her, Julia made an alligator with a wide-open pink mouth and gross yellow teeth. Of Julia's wiggly, vertical balloon Sally made a tree with birds in their nests. "El's right," Julia said. "You are a good artist. Is that what you want to be when you grow up?"

Something inside Sally clanged. Nobody had ever called her an artist, yet by that clang she knew that's exactly what she was. She nodded and ducked close to her paper, abashed and wildly pleased.

Julia said, "Good. You and me. We'll be the artists in the family—agreed?"

Sally has thought of this moment a thousand times since.

An oven door twanged in the kitchen and pots were shoved around on a stove. Randi and a couple of other people were cooking. Julia and Sally drew new squiggles for each other. Down the long table, beside jars of honey and jams, a fat gray tiger cat flicked its tail perilously close to a plate of melting yellow butter. Sally turned her paper sideways and made the big S Julia had given her into that cat. "Clever," Julia said. "So tell me, Pips, will your folks make Ellis go home with them?"

"Probably," she said. "They're afraid he won't go to college."

"Of course he's going to college," Julia said. "We were going to drive down next week and camp along the way." She stilled, listening to the murmur from upstairs. "We wanted to spend our last few days together." She lifted her arms to tighten her ponytail and Sally wondered when she, too, would have lovely curls under her arms.

Ellis called to Julia to come upstairs. Of the scrawl of coils and points Sally had given her, Julia had drawn a long-haired girl atop a tower.

Sally couldn't find Katie anywhere, so she petted the big dogs—her mom still had Hinky—and examined some dusty seashells on a window ledge till someone rang a triangle. Her parents and Ellis and Julia came downstairs, and six or so other people appeared, and the people in the kitchen. They crammed around the long table on stools and plastic lawn chairs and a picnic table bench two of the guys lugged in. Everyone was around Julia's age, except for a couple who were older, though not as old as Sally's parents. The cooks brought out a salty soup with green onions floating on top that you sipped from bowls—no spoons! After that came a loaf thing made of nuts and beans that looked and tasted like dirt, and some beets, ditto; then a weed salad that tasted, well, like weeds, sour and peppery. Ellis ate everything—Ellis, who wouldn't touch a vegetable at home.

"It's Ellis's last supper," said the older man. "We hate to see him go. But the man has baseball to play. We'll see you in the majors, brother! To Ellis!"

And everyone raised pint mason jars full of a tea made from twigs. "Ellis!"

On their way out of town, they stopped at the Kandy Kone so Ellis could tell the people there that he was leaving. His boss, a short bald man, came out to the van and invited them in for ice cream. They left with their cones—their mother said they had no time and miles to go. The boss gave Ellis money and kissed the side of his head.

Ellis stretched out in the far back seat and put a pillow over his face. That meant Sally had to share the middle seat with Katie, but Katie was not as annoyed as she usually was because she was dying to tell Sally what she'd found out. Katie had hidden in the bathroom next to where their parents talked to Ellis and she'd heard everything. She cupped Sally's ear and whispered into it. "Mom said Julia could be arrested because Ellis wasn't eighteen when they started living together. Ellis said if that happened, Mom and Dad would never see him again for the rest of their lives. Then Dad said that if Ellis came home with us now he could phone Julia anytime he wanted—though Mom said only when the rates were low. Dad said Julia could come for Thanksgiving, he'd buy her a ticket. Dad also said that Ellis could save all his ice cream store money, that they'd pay all his expenses that the scholarship didn't cover. But only if he came with us now. Ellis said he and Julia planned to come down next week anyway and why couldn't they have that time together? Mom said they couldn't trust him after he'd been incommunicado all summer. Then Ellis went to get Julia and Mom and Dad argued. Dad said that Ellis should stay, that he was having a wonderful summer and he should finish his job at the Kandy Kone. Mom said that Julia would brainwash him into blowing off Ole Miss—hadn't she already gotten him to hide from his family for three months? Dad said, only two months. And Julia was too much of a rebel, Mom said—didn't he see? All the black hair on her legs? After a while, Ellis brought Julia upstairs. Dad talked to her out in the hall and then Ellis did—I didn't hear any of that, but Ellis agreed to come home so long as he could call Julia whenever he wanted, even during the day. Then Julia made a little speech about how she didn't want our parents to be mad at her because she and Ellis truly loved one another and would be together forever, and she hoped to love and be loved by his family, too."

Sally thought then, *So that's where Ellis got all that love talk.*

At home, Ellis shaved off his beard. His chin was pink and inflamed and his eyes had a new, weird light. He spent a lot of time on the phone with Julia, and also in Sally's room, sitting against the bed with Hinky on his lap while she colored on the floor. He talked to Sally about Julia because Sally was the only person in the family who liked her. Sally more than liked her; she wanted to be her: calm and kind and an artist. Ellis said when Julia finished college in two years, they'd probably get married.

Having Ellis home didn't make Sally's mother any happier. She kept on yanking things, including Sally—"Get off the damn floor, Sal!"—and kept harping about how big the phone bill would be.

"I said I'd pay it," Ellis yelled. "Just tell me how much."

One night Ellis wouldn't come to the dinner table.

"All I said was, he'd get over her," Sally's mother said. "That once he got to college, he'd meet girls who were much more his speed."

"Why would you even say such a thing?" her father said.

Ellis was with them for only six days before he left for Mississippi. They were not happy days for him, though Hinky and Sally loved having him there. Their parents had bought him a standby ticket and once he found out he could use it anytime, he left a week earlier than planned, when he found out he could get into the dorms. Sally's father said, "We've barely had any time with him," but her mother said, "The sooner he's there, the better I'll feel."

They took him to the airport as a family. There were no security checks then and you could walk right to the gate and wave till your traveler disappeared down the gangway. "Bye, Little Squeaks," Ellis said to Sally. "Take care of yourself and Hinky."

"Bye, Ellis!" she called. "See you in the funny papers!"

Five days later, on a Sunday afternoon, someone from Ole Miss phoned their parents. Ellis and some of his dorm mates had gone swimming in an old granite quarry; he dove into the water and never came up. Someone had dumped a load of trees there illegally and Ellis got snarled in the branches and couldn't get free. The police had to bring in heavy equipment to pull the trees away to get his body out.

Sally's father flew to Mississippi and was gone for two days.

Her mother was in her room and Katie was at her friend Christine's house when her father came home. Sally ran to the kitchen to greet him. He stood at the table in his rumpled seersucker summer suit, his suitcase at his feet. He was flipping through the mail; stacks of letters and magazines and junk mail. Already some condolence cards had come. "I missed you, Sally, hon," her father said, and bent to hug her. He smelled as he always did coming home from a trip, a sour smoky mix of cigarettes, oily food, and whiskey. He'd brought a present: on the table by all the mail sat a box wrapped in shiny ivory paper and tied with a thick purple ribbon. For a bright moment, Sally hoped it was for her. Oh, but it was probably candy, and for everyone, another big assortment of chocolates he'd bought at the airport. When he picked up his suitcase and went down the hall to see her mother, Sally took a closer look. A typed paper label was pasted on one end of the box. It was Ellis. That was how the crematorium had packaged him, and how their father had carried him home.

Julia at Twenty

Julia set out at sunrise from her mother's house in Oakland, taking the middle route, the 101, for scenery, but she had forgotten about Gilroy and the garlic stink for miles. She held her breath.

"Why not just call and tell them?" her mother had asked.

What Julia had to say seemed too momentous, too formal for a phone call, and there wasn't enough time for a letter. She had till Monday. She needed to think. She could think on the long drive. And again on the drive back. So she steered her '68 VW bug south through the coastal hills still golden dry from summer heat and dotted with brooding dark oaks.

"One thing's for sure," her mother had said. "I won't raise it."

The flatland fields around Salinas were muddy furrows or the roiling greens of lettuce and broccoli. The midmorning traffic was thick. Julia had to concentrate, downshift, change lanes.

Early on, she and Ellis had talked about what they would do if this happened. They were drinking coffee on one of the ratty dog-haired sofas on the porch at Bug Hollow with the Doberman mix drowsing between them. She'd felt bloated and she was late. It wasn't the right time, they agreed: college counted most. They'd take care of it. That was legal now—unlike when Julia's mother was a girl. In fact, the university health center could refer her, which she knew because of a friend sophomore year. Anyway, she'd bled the next day. False alarm.

What would Ellis say now?

The dead don't talk.

So weird how history repeats," her mother said.

Julia's twenty-year-old father had married his pregnant seventeen-year-old girlfriend while on leave; four months later, while transporting Chinese ex-prisoners of war to Formosa, he and over two dozen other Marines perished when their landing craft collided with another one in a South Korean harbor.

Her parents' story did not exactly align with Julia's, which was more like: Ellis died and three months later, just when she was pulling out of it (that is, when she'd met someone else), she found out.

Before that had come the weeks of flattening shock, obsessive looping memories, Ellis's death reabsorbed and wept for again and again. At twenty, crying hurt; it hurt like vomiting, a painful wrenching. And along with grief had come a new horror of life—a revulsion, really. How weird life was, how absolute, how irremediable: imagine Ellis, Ellis of all people, *Ellis* gone for eternity.

She had to be careful, even now, as she shifted up to fourth gear on the open highway again, to not reinfect herself with that sticky, toxic terror that life—*this* life, which gave you the beautiful sparkling world—squashed you like a gnat.

Two weeks after Ellis died, she'd left her summer home at Bug Hollow and moved with college friends into a rental in Aptos—a dump but it allowed dogs. Back at school, she took Backgrounds of Contemporary Architecture, Renaissance Art, and Painting 2.0, and the health center shrinks (first the psychologist, then the prescribing psychiatrist) steadied her with pills and patient assurances (*Life is worth living!*). *Emotionally labile* was written on her chart—she'd peeked. Labile. Liplike. The art department assigned her to a studio and there she painted lips, grids of them. Lip after lip in muted Morandi colors, thirty-six, forty-eight to a canvas board. She painted between classes, through dinnertime, till two or four in the morning, each brushstroke posing the next problem to solve, until the smell of linseed oil began to nauseate her, and she switched to acrylics, which were stiff and unyielding but odorless.

Sharing her studio was the new TA, Hugo Lopez-Rafael, who played ska and rockabilly and Jonathan Richman and cooked quesadillas on his electric frying pan, always making enough for her, leaving off any meat and then the pico de gallo when onions and garlic became intolerable; when coffee lost its appeal he introduced her to atole. (And still she never suspected.) Hugo's eyes were dark and shining and she painted them, too: grids of welling vortices in warm, dark umbers, sepias, and blacks. Weeks, then a month, then another month passed, and the plummets eased off; she could go half a day, then a whole day, then days without sickening swoops into the abyss. Her chest was still tender from all that weeping when Hugo finally kissed her.

Because they'd kissed—well, a little more than that—she went to student health for a pelvic and pap and a new diaphragm. The gyno cupped her uterus from within. "You know about this, right?"

She did not. She'd had periods, light ones—well, irregular spotting that she took for another by-product of sorrow, like her dwindling appetite and food aversions. She'd never been sick in *the mornings*. Though her breasts were tender.

She was three months in, the doctor said, *at least*. Again, he cupped, then lifted her womb and she saw the shape, like an upturned bowl.

She had a decision to make, and fast. For removal—the doctor's term—she had till Monday. Which was already pushing it. Any later, they'd have to induce. "Make the appointment," the nurse said after the gyno left. "Take the weekend to think it through. You can always cancel."

She'd wiped off the KY jelly, dressed, and on her way out of the clinic got the referral number and right there made an appointment for Monday at one p.m. In her car, she said, "Jesus Christ, Ellis," then drove to her mother's house in Oakland.

The difference is," said her mother, "you won't keep it."

No. Not for a second did Julia think of keeping it. She had no desire to be a mother, not now. Her childhood had been a lived screed against single parenthood.

Only in the past four years had her pretty, not yet forty-year-old mother settled into steady, well-paid work as a court recorder.

A glimpsed fantasy—a house full of sunlight and baby smells, a high chair, a crib, a hot and tightly swaddled being—failed to take hold. She'd choose college any day, and the painting studio with its concrete chill and solvent reek.

"I made an appointment."

"Good. See that you keep it, sweetie."

"You had me."

"And never regretted it, my love. But that's not the life I want for you."

"But, but," she stuttered, "it's like the last bit of El hanging on for dear life. I'd feel so guilty. Like I'd finished him off once and for all."

"So, what, then? You'd have it?"

"And give it up. I don't know."

"Going full term is a big damn deal," said her mother. "On your body and your life. You'd have to leave school for the last few months at least. And for what?"

She called Hugo and told him. Hugo, the raised-Catholic, was silent for a long time. She imagined his sperm bumping up against her big round womb: no admittance. She'd have to paint that. "I bet his folks would want it," he said finally. "Ellis's folks."

She'd thought of that too. "But could you bear me all fat and pregnant with a dead man's baby?"

"Could you bear it?" said Hugo.

Ellis's folks. She'd met them last August when they came to fetch him from Bug Hollow. The mom was a sourpuss. She'd kept the family dog on a short leash the whole time. And she'd accused Julia of kidnapping and brainwashing her son; she'd called Bug Hollow a commune and a cult.

How the other Bug Hollow residents laughed when Julia told them this! The ramshackle, uninsulated nineteenth-century lodge in the Santa Cruz Mountains was a white elephant that her art history professor had inherited and couldn't afford. He rented rooms to students over the summer, which paid the property taxes and gave seven or eight college kids a few months in the woods.

She'd met Ellis and his friends at the beach and brought them home for the night. The friends left the next day, and Ellis stayed. Hiding from his parents was his idea. His brattiness. He called them and wrote to them but wouldn't tell them where he was. "If they ever find out, they'll be up here in a snap!"

Right he was! Some neighbor lady saw the missing-person ad and narced, and shortly the whole family arrived in a VW camper: grouchy mom, bored teenager, eight-year-old Pips, and kind, gentle dad.

Who had taken her aside, and said he was so happy to meet her, and hoped to get to know her better over time. If she could convince Ellis to come home with them, that would mean so much after their long summer of worry. She and Ellis could talk whenever they wanted, "phone bill be damned." And he'd send her a ticket to join the family for Thanksgiving.

Join the family.

"Let's think long term here." The father's large brown eyes were affectionate, his voice low, conspiratorial. "His mom's been heartsick and frantic. She's all wound up. Not herself. But—strategically speaking—you'd do well to humor her; I mean, if you and Ellis are together for the long haul—and I hope you are, Julia—she's the nut you'll have to crack."

The mom's cap of mink-brown hair and round, deeply tanned face did suggest a nut, an acorn or a filbert.

Julia did not know of fathers, but this one seemed—a word swam to mind—a *prince.*

She and Ellis had planned to camp down the coast, which still would have given him a week with his family before he left for Ole Miss. But she told him to go. "Let's be strategic, here," she said. "Let's think long term. If your parents are ever to accept me . . ."

But—and she had to be very careful even circling this idea—if she had held on to him for that extra week, he might not have gone to Ole Miss on quite the same time schedule, and he might not have gone swimming when he had, and he might be telling her now, *Hey, college counts the most.*

She had not gone to Altadena for the memorial service, although the dad offered her a ticket to LAX.

The service was less than a week after Ellis died, and then they'd sit shiva, whatever that meant. Too much too soon! ("Yes, but it's how Jews traditionally deal with death," her mother said. "Quickly. Though I'm surprised he was cremated. I thought Jews didn't do that.") Julia had wanted to go, she thought she should, but how to dress, pack, get on a plane, then hold it together among strangers when she sobbed involuntarily, convulsively, and her eyes were swollen, and the terrible knowledge flooded her at odd moments that the worst could and did happen, and the most clever, graceful boy, the very one you chose and adored, who woke you with kisses, could disappear forever.

She thought of him down there, in the tree's grip, pushing, shoving, fighting the urge to take a breath and finally filling his lungs with cool blue water.

She knew when it happened. When they were out of jelly. Barely a smear for her diaphragm. Early in August. Right around the eighth, his eighteenth birthday. His last birthday.

The highway left the sparkling ocean and its glinting mist and veered inland, where it was overcast. She would not see water again for hours, till Pismo.

They'd only been together two months. Ellis had been dead longer than that already.

In a few miles, the gray clouds began breaking apart and great shafts of sun shone through like a prophecy: *All will be well.*

She had to pull over twice and breathe into a paper bag—the psychologist had shown her that. It was an old doughnut bag, sweet, with shards of icing.

Hugo was sweet. Roly-poly. Pudgy. Sexy. Beautiful caramel skin. Thick black hair to his shoulders. No beard to speak of. A little older. Twenty-four. A terrific dancer. He clasped her firmly, expertly. He held on. He saw her sadness and set out to ease it.

Ellis had been much younger, so young, and so slim, it was like embracing a long-waisted skinny girl. A solidly muscled, lively girl. He had a slow quirky smile and a quick eye. He was silly with the dogs. And god, the sweetest kisser ever. Yet so disciplined, training every day. The sit-ups the push-ups the chin-ups and leg lifts; the planks and five-mile runs; the hours of pitching practice. He could detonate a tomato on a fence post with a baseball from sixty feet.

He knew how to look at paintings, too, and talk about them. Nobody had ever given her work as much attention (not even Hugo). "Our mom took us to art museums," Ellis said, "and made us stand in front of one painting for twenty minutes and say everything we saw."

Imagine a mother like that, however grouchy. Or a family like that: with music lessons, museums, day trips, camping. Her own childhood was a blur of boredom and apprehensive waiting, with her mother working multiple jobs, a neighbor checking in.

Two months and seven days was all she'd had of Ellis. The psychologist asked, Could she see that time as *one of life's fleeting gifts*? "And be grateful for what you had?"

Yes, yes, though now she was not so grateful for the cells colonizing her womb.

She was selfish; she wanted to paint and to have a gallery by the time she graduated and rent a downtown studio with Hugo.

She would not drop out of school like her mother had; if need be, she'd squat in the painting studio and push it out there. She didn't *want* an abortion. But who does?

She didn't *want* to carry full term and go through labor, either.

There was something creepy, *gothic*, about carrying a dead guy's kid.

Her wants were off the table. *So let's think long term here. Strategically.*

Oh, the father. And the low sorrow in his voice when he said, "Is this Julia? It's Phil, Phil Samuelson, Ellis's father. I'm afraid I have some very sad news. Is someone there with you?" She was in Bug Hollow's den, on the downstairs phone, so she sat in the armchair placed there for conversations, where she'd lolled and talked to Ellis for hours. Yes, yes, she said, already trembling. Many people and dogs were nearby. Ubu the white shepherd mix wandered up then; she placed a staying hand on his ruff. And the father said, "Your beloved, your Ellis had an accident today. He dove into a quarry pond and he got stuck in some logs and couldn't get free. And I'm so sorry to tell you, Julia, dear, he drowned." And the father had sobbed. "We lost him, Julia. He's gone."

She'd pushed her face into the shepherd's dusty dog-smelling fur.

Bug Hollow held its own memorial for Ellis. Nine of them stood in a circle in the backyard and everyone had a flower, a wildflower, and one by one they placed their flower in the center jar and said something about Ellis. *Best pitching arm ever . . . Sweet man . . . So fucking smart . . .* She said, *Oh, god, how he kissed. And laughed!* Then they fanned out and played a long round of catch and while the hard ball flew among them, stinging their bare palms, the wind came up. "There's Ellis," someone said.

Later, her mother said oh yes, the wind often comes up at memorials.

Lone farmhouses sat far apart in the fields she passed and set off the familiar ache of her endless childhood. Thousands of hours alone.

If she gave them the baby, then what? Could she be like a distant cousin, appearing at Thanksgiving and Easter? Why not be Ellis's old girlfriend, still close to the family, coming for a holiday visit? In memoriam. To see how the kid was faring.

Hugo, who grew up in Oxnard, had told her about a hot spring near Gaviota, how to find it, where to park. "It will relax and energize you," he said. Her mother was dubious: "Some bacteria might get up there. . . ." Some bacteria could be the answer to everything. Taking a rutted trail up the steep hillside, she followed a couple. Shawled with towels, with matching long straggly hair, they trudged like religious pilgrims. She had no towel. Her hair was cut short, like a boy's. The day she'd left Bug Hollow she stopped at the barbershop in Boulder Creek and had the barber shave it up the back. Now it was growing in as short, bumpy tufts.

Amazing that Hugo found her at all attractive.

The hot spring was a steaming dark pool, the banks trampled black clay. Heads bobbed in the white vapor, some faces were smeared with that clay. A thin man, his whole body clay-covered and dried to a crusty ash color, crouched on the bank and smoked a joint, his dangling genitals a startling pink. Julia stripped, her belly already a hard little mound—that upturned bowl—while the rest of her was bony, her ribs xylophonic. She hadn't been truly hungry for months.

The water was hot and stinging and smelly, the late-afternoon air cool. The steam made her cough, her toes sank in gooshy mud. Julia found a place to dig soft clay from the bank and smeared her own face. She wished Hugo was here now, so they could be like the couple she'd followed: the woman resting against the man's chest, her breasts floating amid snaky strands of hair. As Julia watched, up rose the pale dome of the woman's belly, a pale, much larger bowl than her own.

She dried off with her checkered cowboy shirt, then put it back on. Poking along in traffic as she neared Santa Barbara, she smelled herself. The ocean blazed like a giant opal. Her face glowed pink and she reeked like a rotten egg. Like a sulfurous fart. A sniff of hell.

She pulled into a gas station in Pasadena to ask directions to the Samuelsons' address. The attendant looked in a book of maps and wrote out the turns. In the deep blue twilight, she came to the street of modest ranch houses and older clapboard cottages. Ellis's home stood out: a modernist experiment, designed and built, she knew, by the engineer father. The red-and-black VW van was in the driveway behind a small yellow Toyota sedan.

She'd thought they were richer. And wished she didn't reek of brimstone.

At the turquoise front door, she took a breath. Inside, a dog began barking. She knocked and waited. How would she tell them? Would she just blurt it?

"Oh for crying out loud." The dad was already stepping back so she could enter. His starched white dress shirt crumpled as he hugged her. The long-legged prancing dog leapt around them. Hinky!

"Oh, Hinky," she said and crouched, offering her face to be licked.

"Who is it, Phil?" the mother called, although now they were already through the kitchen, and she could see. "Who is that? Is that you . . . uh . . ."

"It's me, Mrs. Samuelson. Julia."

"Your hair!" The mother—the nut to crack—looked frantically to her husband, as if for explanation.

And across the table sat the younger sister, Sally—Pip, Ellis had called her. His favorite. Lovely Little Pip, whose eyes, huge behind her glasses, shone with surprise and delight. *Hi*, they mouthed to each other, *Hi!*

The family sat on barstools at a Formica tabletop built around a stovetop—a modern cook 'n' serve arrangement. Places were set for four but only the mom, dad, and Pip were there—weird: Had they known she was coming?

"Have you eaten? Take Katie's seat. She's having dinner at a friend's."

Between the mom and dad, Julia slipped off her leather jacket, releasing a burst of warm sulfured air. The mother's nostrils contracted.

"Sorry. I went to a hot spring." Nobody registered this, and she gave up.

They seemed so quiet, so separate from one another.

Maybe she wouldn't tell them. Maybe this was one big wrong turn.

The mother gulped from a green plastic tumbler filled with dark liquid.

The father spooned mashed potatoes on a plate. "Pork chop?"

She shook her head. A little spinach, yes. *How ordinary they seemed, and pale!* So diminished from the family that had trooped into Bug Hollow to claim their missing fifth.

Looking and not looking at her, they waited for her to explain herself. She ate some grainy potatoes and watery greens. Sliced iceberg in a white plastic bowl was pushed her way, but garlic wafted from the dressing.

Little Pip sculpted her mashed potatoes into a rectangle and sneaked shy glances. Ellis had adored this sister; she was constantly creative, he said. "You remind me of her," he'd told Julia. "Funny and sweet and always making stuff." Once, he said, he watched for an hour as six-year-old Pip made a pair of shoes from Naugahyde scraps, cardboard, a hole punch, and yarn. At Bug Hollow, while the parents were browbeating Ellis into coming home, Julia had kept Pip company; they'd drawn pictures together, and it was cozy and easy, as if they already knew each other through both loving Ellis.

Pip—and the dad—were the only ones who'd made an effort to know her that day.

At least the baby would have those two.

So she should tell them.

But once she did, there'd be no going back. If only the parents—the mother—were warmer, more . . . *familial.* Of course, sorrow had sapped them, blanched them, isolated them, even from one another. Or maybe it was the tube light shivering overhead. Still, something must be said. "I wanted to see you guys." Hearing a false chirp in her voice, she added, "I'm sorry I missed the memorial service."

The mother grabbed Julia's hand. Her rings pinched Julia's fingers.

"We knew it was awfully hard for you," the father said. His white shirt had an oily orange smudge under the pocket. "We understood."

Julia slowly pulled her hand from the mother's grip and

joined it to her other hand under the table. "Sorry to just show up. I wanted to see where he grew up."

Where a child might be raised.

The mother looked up sharply. "Of course you'll stay the night. You can have Sally's room if you can stand the mess," she said. "And you'll want a shower after such a long drive."

They had stingy scrapings of Neapolitan ice cream for dessert, then the mom and Little Pip took her through the living room with its high, stained-gray wood beams, sliding glass doors, pleated drapes. A grand piano dominated one corner. She'd imagined a larger, homier home. A wealthier one. Then again, she assumed most intact families with a professional, working dad were wealthy.

In the hall, the mother opened a door, flipped on a light. "We haven't touched a thing," she said, and nudged Pip along so Julia would be alone.

Sports trophies and toy trucks sat on shelves with old textbooks. Well-used hardballs nested in two child-size mitts. Front pages of yellowing sports sections—*Dodgers Triumph! Dodgers Take Series!*—were Scotch-taped right to the wall. (Her mother would never allow tape on a wall!) The bed was covered with boxes; one held pieces of a train set. In another were folded clothes, and on top was the faded gray T-shirt with the Aztec calendar that Ellis wore all last summer. She touched the frazzled collar. She was glad they hadn't wanted her to sleep in here.

"Take it." The teenage girl stood at the door, her dark hair French-braided, her mouth bristling with braces. Katie.

"I have a few of his T-shirts at home," Julia said. A lie; she'd thrown them out.

Katie looked hard at her. "But take anything else you want. I'm sure it's fine."

"That's okay." Julia surveyed the room. If the yellow walls became a soft, clean white, a changing table could go under the window there, and where the bed was, a crib. Above that, maybe a mobile of origami birds, slowly spinning.

In the bathroom mirror, she saw black mud in her hairline and in a crease of her neck. No wonder the mother suggested a shower. In the spray she scrubbed herself fiercely and twice used the harsh green shampoo in a see-through tube.

They might not want a baby from her, the filthy urchin. Which would be less bother for everyone. She had her appointment. By Monday night, all would be over.

A mad urge arose then, to run wet and naked, belly first, and announce.

But really, why hurry? She could take more time to decide; it just meant she'd go through labor to end it—though surely not so intense a labor as full-term birth.

Though if you had to go through labor at all, why not produce a living thing?

I tried to clean up." Indeed, Pip had shoved a considerable pile of little girl's clothes, books, shoes, toys, and art supplies into the corner by her closet. Still, small dirty socks littered the kid-size desk along with crayons, picture books, a naked baby doll, plastic barrettes.

Her mother had never allowed Julia's room to get like this. A little girl's mess.

"It's fine, lovely." In her nightie, her hair in a towel, Julia sat on the bed. The mother had already put on clean sheets. "Come sit." She patted the corded red bedspread. "Did you do those?" Bright drawings of faces, animals, flowers, and houses were Scotch-taped to the opposite wall. The girl's strong use of color, her confident lines and jaunty shapes were so playful, so advanced for her age. Best of all were the lively, antic expressions on the faces, human and animal. "I love them!"

"I'm going to be an artist when I grow up, like you."

"You already are," said Julia.

The girl snuggled closer. She gave off heat. Her fine dun-colored hair floated in the least puff of air. In Julia's chest, that old soreness, formed from the hardest sobs, ached. What if this was what she was making—a Pip-like person? "Tell me, sweetheart. Was it okay growing up in your house?"

Pip's small pink fingers tangled in her lap. "It was okay. Till Ellis."

"It's been so sad and hard, I know. But your folks are nice."

"My dad is. And Hinky. My mom's so sad, she's mad all the time."

"I imagine she's terribly sad. You all must be. But you used to have good times together, right? Ellis said you guys were always going camping and to movies and museums and concerts. That was fun, wasn't it?"

"Concerts are boring," said Sally. "So are operas."

Julia had never been to an opera. "You know, Pip, you were Ellis's favorite sister."

She nodded solemnly. "He always used to say that. And he said you'd be my sister when you guys got married."

"Sister-in-law," Julia said. "I would have liked that so much."

"Yes, but . . ." Sally nudged her.

Katie stood in the doorway. "Sally," she said, "Mom says you have to go to bed."

Pip hugged Julia's neck, kissed her wetly on the mouth, and ran out. Katie, too, turned to leave.

"How're you doing, Katie?" said Julia.

"How do you think?" Katie, looking back, bared her braces. "It was bad enough when Ellis ran away, but now? It's like God took a giant shit right in the middle of our house."

Julia rubbed her still-wet hair with the towel and finger-combed it. In the white cotton nightie she'd brought, her nipples stuck out like nailheads, so she pulled on the checkered shirt again to go say good night to the parents. *She'd tell them in the morning. Maybe she would. Or not.* Halfway down the hall, she heard Katie's loud angry voice. "Of course she's knocked up. Why else would she come here? I mean look at her. She sure didn't have those boobs last August."

Julia's first impulse was to dash back to Pip's bedroom, grab her knapsack, and slip out the front door. So it would be as if she'd never come.

The father caught up to her before she reached Pip's door. "Julia, honey," he said, and for the second time that evening, he held her.

The mother: "Of course we want it, of course we want Ellis's baby—it is Ellis's, you're sure?"

"And mine," said Julia.

"You haven't done any drugs, have you?" The mother again.

The father said, "Let's just slow down here. . . ."

He took over the questions. Health insurance? (She had a college health plan, and was also on her mother's policy.) School? (Her mother was right: she'd probably have to take off spring quarter.) Financial support? (Some would be helpful once her scholarship paused.) What else?

"If you take it," she said, "would I still get to see her or him from time to time?"

The mother said, "I'm not sure that's a good—"

The dad: "Let's see what feels right as we go along."

"I want everything completely legal and straightforward," said the mother.

"I'd like that too," said Julia.

They'd find a good adoption lawyer, the father said, and be in touch.

When they arrived six weeks later, the lawyer's letter and preliminary forms were a shock: Julia must agree to terminate all parental rights.

The official papers would be signed after the baby was born, though she would have forty-eight hours after the birth to change her mind. Even then, it would be six to eight months until the adoption was finalized by a judge.

She called Phil Samuelson at his work number. "I was hoping maybe I could see her—or him—sometimes, like I was a family friend or something. Not like a mother or anything."

He said not to worry, that once the adoption was final, they'd work out something. "I'm sure we can give you updates and photos," he said. "This was just the least complicated way to go. Though Sib is worried that it will confuse the child to have another mother showing up from time to time. Of course, we also won't lie to the child about where they came from."

She'd had the same thoughts and equivocations. Only one thing was certain: she would not keep it. That door was shut.

———

As months passed, she did have regrets—fleeting ones—about going through with the pregnancy, as it was taking a very long time and her body felt other, occupied, ungainly. Fat. Her organs were squished up against her lungs and spine. She leaked. She kept her weight down for months, so when she finally started showing in February, she felt self-conscious, embarrassed in a way she hadn't anticipated, and sat in the back of her classrooms, leaving early. But she was never impatient or angry with the fetus. She thought of her—really, she never doubted it was female—as a dear little friend. *We will get you well settled. You'll have a kind dad and one wonderful sister. A mother who will make sure you have a lot of experiences. They will see you through. But Jesus, hurry up.*

She wanted her body, her life to be her own again.

But surely, curiosity would rankle. Both ways.

She rubbed her great, taut, protuberant belly. *One day, we'll meet again.*

She finished the winter quarter and lived in the Aptos house into April. Hugo spent most nights until she was so restless and uncomfortable neither of them slept. His patience and solicitude had begun to burden her. She just wanted to get through this. Her mother suggested she come home to have the baby at Kaiser up there, so Julia moved back into her childhood room in Oakland and waited for the birth.

Eva Ellis Samuelson was born on May 6 at five in the morning after a seven-hour labor that the nurses described as short and easy but that felt neither short nor easy to Julia. Eva was six pounds, two ounces and, like her father, long: almost nineteen inches. She had abundant dark hair, so fine and dense it was more like fur. She and Julia regarded each other blurrily. A great hormonal rush of love swept through Julia, but this was not followed by any great need to possess; she was far too exhausted to revisit her decision. The Samuelsons arrived within hours and came in to see her. Everyone wept and laughed—laughed!—and peered at Eva, passing her around. The father slipped Julia a manila envelope.

Everyone left Julia alone with Eva for a final few minutes. Julia smelled her daughter's neck and cheek, nosed her oddly long, dense, dark hair. "Whenever you're ready, come looking for me," she whispered. "I'll be easy to find. You'll do great with those people. All will be well."

Mother and daughter were discharged at the same time, right around three in the afternoon, and left the hospital in different vehicles.

In the manila envelope, Julia found a painting in tempera by Little Pip of a smiling Hinky-like dog—black with tan eyebrows—standing in deep green grass under a solid, bright blue sky. Also enclosed: a small white envelope with a card and a check. *Here's a little mad money*, the father had written. *Go to Europe, look at paintings. Take a friend.*

Maybe they were richer than she'd thought.

She took her mother. They went first to Florence—to the Accademia and the Uffizi, where, just when the abundance of beatific virgin-and-child paintings had stopped irritating her and begun to depress her, she came across a fourteenth-century wooden altar painting of the annunciation. In the center of a triptych, the kneeling angel Gabriel is focused on Mary with cunning intent; one hand holds an olive branch indicating that he comes in peace, but the other points up to a dove surrounded by angels as if to say, *That dove up there? Whether you like it or not, he is going to impregnate you and it's not any dove, it's God.* His spoken words, clearly meant to butter her up, are in a golden scrawl headed to her ear: *Hail full of grace the Lord is with you.*

Mary, who has a book in her left hand—her thumb is saving her place—reacts like any woman interrupted in her reading and told such news. She cringes, pulls her cloak more tightly closed. Her mouth is a downturned U; she's giving the angel major stink eye. She, clearly, is not with the Lord. So won't he just go away so she can get back to her book?

Julia said to her mother, "At least one painter got it right."

After Florence, they flew to Madrid.

Hugo, who was in Amsterdam for a nine-week summer course, said he'd meet her in Paris; she was to write and tell him when.

In the Prado, she came upon Goya's painting of a dog, or rather, the small head of a dog peering over a ledge or a shore made by a swoop of brown paint across the bottom of the tall canvas. At first, she thought the dog was cute, and that maybe she'd send a postcard of the painting to Little Pip. The longer she looked, though, she grew uneasy. Above the dog stretched a field of mottled ochres and yellows—was it the sky? A body of water? A wall? The dog's ear was made of three quick brush-strokes, its eye was white as if shining, its expression, now that she looked closer, one of appeal. Yes, frantic appeal. Appeal to what? To whom? To the amorphous darkening to its right? In all the cloudy, muddied yellows—and hadn't van Gogh said yellow was God's color?—Julia could almost make out faces, a plunging bird, a human silhouette, but that was mostly wishful thinking. The dog was so small and, she now saw, clearly doomed, the surrounding space so empty and inhospitable. Tears sprang from her eyes. Her chest ached. In fact, she'd never seen any painting so painful and so beautiful. *Goya knew too that life, this beautiful life, is unbearable.*

Her mother came up and, seeing where things stood, slid an arm around Julia's waist. "Enough," she said, and gently pulled her away.

They had to walk through a park to get back to their hotel. Her mother took Julia's hand. "My love," she said. "You might not know it yet, but you have done a very brave, very good, and very generous thing."

That night they went to a large restaurant recommended by the concierge at their hotel. It was loud and noisy, a series of big halls with long tables filling up with families and large, boisterous parties. The menu was extensive, and many—most—of the items they'd never heard of. They studied it and conferred and twice sent away the waiter. A group of Spaniards near them, a party of friends, noticed their confusion. "With only two it is not how to eat here," a woman called to them. "Come, come with us." She and her friends moved to make room, found chairs for them, and passed them plates of grilled sardines, cured meats, cheeses. Olives warmed with whole cloves of garlic and orange skins arrived, and loops of fried squid. Julia, at one end of the table, watched her mother at the other: not yet forty, she was still so pretty, her fair skin with a rosy blush, her thick dark hair bobbed and curly around her face; she was laughing with the young Spanish woman next to her, and eating an octopus leg with her fingers. Julia felt a surge of love for her, and pride in her beauty.

The woman on Julia's right spoke good English—she'd studied architecture in the States; the banker on her left, a man, spoke English haltingly, but was very funny, urging Julia to taste the forkfuls of food he offered—food she otherwise would never ever have touched—as if she were a recalcitrant baby: jambon, slender white anchovies, charred green peppers. So delicious, all of it! Julia must see Toledo, the Spaniards said. And Cuenca. Tomorrow, the architect was driving to Aranjuez—Julia and her mom should come, visit the botanical garden while she was at her meeting; then they could almorzar at a pretty café.

By morning, the expedition was two cars and seven people—some of the young professionals had flexible schedules. Over the weekend, a slightly different configuration drove to Cuenca and spent the night in a hotel hanging over the gorge. Another group formed for a day trip to Toledo.

Julia said to her mother, "I had forgotten fun."

She never did write to Hugo.

A goodbye dinner was held at the large restaurant where they'd all first met. In the morning, with less than a week left before their flight home, she and her mother boarded a train to Paris.

The Teacher

Sib hadn't wanted to take a leave of absence, but her principal, Mrs. Wright, insisted she take two months. During those months, Mrs. Wright invited Sib and her daughters to tea every Saturday afternoon. "You must get out of the house. I know. I have suffered a great loss myself, and I know what it takes to rejoin the living." Often, Sib's best teacher friend, Angela, was also at the teas. In this way, Sib caught up on school news and learned to converse without bursting into tears.

When she returns to the classroom, it's after Thanksgiving.

She has the fourth-grade gifted class at Whitman Elementary. Her long-term sub, Mr. Vadim, is a faded semiretired sixtyish old hand. She met him one afternoon in the faculty lounge, where they went over the material he'd covered in the curriculum. "A lot of really bright kids in the class," he said. "And one boy who doesn't talk."

"What do you mean he doesn't talk?"

"He's an 'elective mute,'" Mr. Vadim said. "His schoolwork is excellent, but he refuses to speak."

Indeed, on her first day back in the classroom when she calls his name during roll—Sandro Grolio—several kids pipe up, "He's here."

They point to a tall boy with a wide soft face. He looks down, unable to meet her gaze.

"He doesn't talk, Mrs. Samuelson," a girl in the front row says quietly.

In the faculty room that first day, the other teachers are deferential and soft-spoken with their greetings. Angela hugs her a little too long—until Sib has to blink back tears. "Okay, everyone," she says gruffly. "What's the deal with Sandro Grolio?"

"He doesn't talk." This was Burt Kunholtz, the third-grade teacher.

"And what's been done about it?" she said.

The special ed teacher, who'd had him for first and second grades, said, "We kept him in special ed, thinking that with extra attention, he'd grow out of it."

"I took him for the third grade and he did fine," said Burt Kunholtz, "except for the not talking. Mrs. Wright had him evaluated. The psychologist diagnosed anxiety and said his IQ was way up there—which is why he's in with your gifteds."

At dinner that night, it's just three of them: her, Phil, and eight-year-old Sally. Katie, their teenager, is having dinner at a friend's. Sib tells Phil and Sally about Sandro.

"His former teachers say he speaks at home, just not at school. And I told them, I said, 'He will by the time I'm done with him!'"

Sally is pushing her dinner into different shapes. She is so close to her plate, her fine dust-colored hair almost touches her food. She's a thousand miles away.

Phil says, "If the kid's so anxious, you might want to go easy."

"What do you think I'm going to do, beat him till he speaks? Sally, please sit up, get your hair off your plate."

Sib has only been teaching school for two years. Before that, she gave private cello lessons three afternoons a week in a room she rented at Sacred Heart, the church closest to her house. When Sally started kindergarten, and when Phil landed the big job at Parsons, Sib went back to school for a master's in early childhood development, then did a year of student teaching for her certificate. By now, she's realized that most of her new colleagues did not hail from the upper percentiles of their college class. (She herself had skipped two grades and graduated summa cum laude from Peabody with a double major in music performance and art history.) That so little has been done to address Sandro's willful muteness she finds appalling, but not surprising: even the youngest, most eager of her coworkers struggle to do the bare minimum.

Sandro is a bit of a lug, a big, shy, mute lug. He radiates discomfort. He eats alone at lunch and reads in the pergola during recesses. In PE, though, he is picked early for the teams—large for his age, he's tall, solid, a good batter and sturdy second baseman. The other boys cheer for him as they do for any teammate. He shows no sign of enjoying or despising any game. Never a smile or a wince.

Sandro is not the only student to snag her interest. The first week she's back, Freddy O'Connor waits after class and shyly asks if she will please let him see her math book—the teacher's edition, with the answers. He has already finished all the chapters on his own and wants to check his work. He shows her a spiral notebook, each exercise neatly numbered, chapter after chapter of them.

She retrieves a fifth-grade math text from the book room and gives it to him and now, on Tuesdays and Thursdays, she tutors him during lunch.

A thin scamp of a boy, Freddy is very bright and funny. Hers is the first gifted class he has ever been placed in. His third-grade teacher, also Mr. Kunholtz, noticed that his score on the state's standardized math test was the highest in the grade, higher than any kid's in the gifted class.

Freddy grasps fractions immediately. *If a 3-pound birthday cake is cut into 24 slices, how much does each slice weigh?* "Not enough for me!" he says. "Two measly ounces!"

On yard duty, out on the playground, she sees that the other smart boys in her class don't include Freddy, or maybe it's that he's still drawn to the boys from his former classes, the average kids. Freddy's dad is a plumber.

Meanwhile, over in the pergola, Sandro sits by himself. He eats his sandwich and apple slices delicately, often touching a paper napkin to his lips. When he's done eating, he unfolds a comic book from his lunch box and reads until the bell rings.

This little math whiz of mine got fractions so fast, it's as if he was born knowing them," Sib announces at the dinner table. "I can't believe nobody noticed till now how bright he is. But they never notice anything. All they do is rush to the faculty room to smoke and gossip. I went into Burt Kunholtz's classroom to borrow some chalk and he has nothing up on the walls, and I mean nothing, just a calendar and the map every class has. No student artwork. Nothing colorful. Those poor kids, sitting there all day with nothing to look at."

Sib gets to work early, usually around seven fifteen. Only she and the janitor are in the building. She mimeographs her handouts in the storeroom. She reviews her lesson plans. She hangs new student work, rearranges her bulletin boards. She feeds the guinea pig and the iguana (she is the only teacher who bothers with pets in the classroom). Then, she settles in with a book, usually a mystery, and her thermos of coffee. The first students straggle in around eight twenty.

On leave, she had a lot of time to herself while the girls were at school, and she got used to it. Now she must steal every minute she can to be alone, especially before the baby comes.

She stays late, too, reshelving books in the class library, tidying up. Socorro, her babysitter/housekeeper, leaves at four thirty, and she tries to make it home by then. But the girls can be by themselves for an hour or two. Katie is fifteen, after all, a babysitter in her own right. And Sally will just be on the floor of her room with her crayons or digging holes under the eucalyptus trees in the Romeros' vacant lot.

Some days, when she turns onto El Pajaro Drive, Sib can't bear to go inside their house. Katie has become a hormone-poisoned, rude, sarcastic teenager, and Sally, well Sally is a little lurker, always spying on Sib, checking on her, and occasionally calling for her so shrilly and in such a panic that Sib is certain the girl is fatally wounded, when usually she just wants to tattle on Katie, who's said something mean, although last week Sally had come across a sluggish gopher snake in the backyard, the tail of a mouse sticking out of its mouth along with one tiny, twitching pink foot.

Once Phil is home, Sib feels less targeted. The girls go to

him for whatever they want—Katie wants to go to her friend Christine's for dinner; Sally wants someone to see yet another new drawing or to help her with a broken shoelace.

If such things overwhelm her now, Sib thinks, what will happen when the baby comes? Time will get even tighter, the demands on her will intensify; she will have to be home earlier, or pay Socorro overtime.

But then, she's always loved a baby. If only they would stay babies.

"We'll get all the childcare you need," Phil assures her. "You have to get used to the idea that we are well off now. Especially since you're working too."

If they are so well off, why can't they move? Leave this house of sadness behind.

Instead of going inside, Sib will park and walk into the neighborhood as the twilight deepens. Or, she'll slip into the house long enough to leash Hinky, their long-legged Manchester terrier, and take her out. Or, she'll drive past the house to halfway around the block where there's a tall oleander hedge, park, and have a good cry.

She calls on students randomly, including Sandro. He doesn't answer and she moves on without comment.

Handing back their papers, Sib often says a word, asks a student a question. She does this with Sandro, waits a bit, and moves on, again without comment.

She phones his home and asks his mother if she can stop by after school.

From an assignment Sandro wrote about his family, Sib knows that they are from Argentina—pushed out, Sib assumes, by the junta—and that he is the youngest of six, with three sisters and two brothers. His father owned a department store in Córdoba, Argentina, but here he works in his brother's TV-repair shop.

The Grolios live about five blocks from Whitman Elementary on a quiet street of modest, close-together older homes. Theirs is a ramshackle clapboard bungalow in need of paint or a good scrub. Most likely it's a rental. The front lawn is crisp crabgrass, with two kid-size goal nets for soccer. Sib crosses a wide covered porch to knock.

As she opens the door, Mrs. Grolio motions her over to where she has set out folding chairs and a card table on the porch. "More privacy here," she says.

Sib was hoping to get a good look inside, but she'll have to settle for what she can see through the plateglass window: sweaters and coats flung on a sofa, a few books leaning on built-in shelves. Mrs. Grolio brings out a tray with coffee, cups, and plain brown biscuits. She is a tall, angular woman with short black curls and a nose that comes out of her forehead, like a woman in a Picasso drawing. "Yes, Sandro talks at home," she says, pouring coffee. "He has no problem with English—with the kids, English is all they speak."

"But Sandro never talks to anyone except here at home, right?"

"He talks at his cousins' house." She waves down the street.

"Have you ever asked him why he won't talk at school?"

"He was scared at first. Now, it's just what he does."

"Did something set it off?"

"Kids teased him. They called him Mexican." She takes a biscuit. "So much was new for him—new school, new country, so many new rules nobody explained."

"That is a lot." Matriculations are scary, Sib thinks. She herself was so anxious on her first day of graduate school that Phil drove her to USC, walked her to class, then came back to pick her up. She adds, "A lot of change for a little kid."

"A lot of change for all of us," the mother said. "In Argentina, I was a buyer for our store; I traveled to New York, London, all over Europe. Here, until the green card, I clean houses."

The mother's English is excellent, with a light, melodic accent. Her straight gray wool skirt and red sweater do seem like professional clothes demoted to at-home wear.

A scuffling within the house rouses Sib: two dark-eyed, dark-haired adolescent girls peer at her through the plate glass; seen, they thud off with wallops of laughter.

"It's just that Sandro's always by himself at school. I worry that he's lonely."

"Sandro? Sandro's not lonely! He has his sisters and brothers and cousins!" Again, she waves at some house down the street. "They play every day."

"Also, Mrs. Grolio, if he doesn't start talking, it could hurt his chances later, getting into Advanced Placement classes. Or into a good college."

"Mrs. Samuelson," she says. "Sandro is nine years old. School is not the most important thing in his life. We are. His family. Here, with us, he's a happy kid. He will figure things out. If advanced classes and college are important to him, maybe he will start talking. But I can't make him. It's up to him."

On Saturday mornings, Sib does the week's shopping. At the door, she calls, without urgency, "Girls, I'm going out now. Anyone coming with?"

These days, only Sally ever does.

Sib dislikes supermarkets, the shivering fluorescent light, the long aisles and crowded shelves, the endless choices, so she makes a round of smaller stores; first Preble's, the fancy produce market in a chilly warehouse where fruits and vegetables are still in their field crates; then the cheerful butcher on Lake Avenue, the little Armenian market with the best coffee, and finally the Italian market for lunch meat and noodles.

Today at Preble's, Sally wants Sib to buy purple potatoes. "Let's have them with corn and carrots, it will be so pretty!" she says.

Sib, amused, thinks, *Who is this person?* and buys a pound.

Sally has always loved food, especially strong tastes; as a toddler, she devoured olives and pickles; at eighteen months, she once ate a whole jar of mustard. Phil and Sib had watched, curious to see how far she'd go.

In the Armenian store, Sally begs for the lahmajune covered with za'atar, and at the Italian store, when the counterman gives her a sliver of hard cheese with peppercorns in it, she wants Sib to buy some of that, too.

At almost nine, Sally's becoming long-waisted and skinny, like Ellis was. Too bad she doesn't have his thick, curly, corn-yellow hair; hers is a lackluster dishwater blond so fine and fly-away that even the smallest rubber bands slip out of it. And it snarls horribly, especially during the night, the knots sometimes so dense Sib has to cut them out. But Sally insists on keeping her hair long and only agreed to a pixie cut once after a disastrous home perm. Sib had carefully layered the plastic rollers—a headache given the spiderweb nature of Sally's hair—until, bored and irritated at how long it was taking, she stopped being so meticulous. Predictably, one side came out a fuzz ball, with the other barely waved. Sally let the hairdresser cut it short but in the car home she'd sobbed into her fingers.

That was before they really had something to cry about.

After they've finished their rounds, Sib drives up into the San Rafael Hills to look at the houses for sale. With well-groomed yards and winding streets, San Rafael is a neighborhood Sib could happily live in. Phil won't even discuss moving, let alone go house-hunting with her.

She and Sally have a game. They stop at For Sale signs, and if there are flyers, Sally will dash out and take one. Sib will ask the number of bedrooms and the square footage, then guess the price. If she's within five thousand dollars, Sally will say, "You win, Mom"; otherwise, it's "Close, Mom," or "Way, way off, Mom."

Phil doesn't want to move because he designed and built their house on El Pajaro. He was building it when Sib met him almost twenty years ago—that was part of what charmed her. He had studied with and then worked for the architect Gregory Ain, who built a street of modernist houses a mile to the east. Phil had loved those houses so much, he'd designed one for himself using Ain's signature elements—open kitchens, clerestories, white rock roofs.

Sib, too, loved the house, and its large lot subdivided from a lemon grove. Phil's mother lived around the corner then—and Sib loved her, too. The two women had coffee every afternoon when the kids were young. Coffee with a dunk of something. They talked and laughed and watched the kids play. They never ran out of things to talk about. But Phil's mother has been dead for three years, and now, since Ellis's accident, the whole neighborhood seems dingy with sadness. Sib wants someplace new and different—perhaps this half-timbered cottage with a hard-pruned rose garden. Sally bolts out and grabs a flyer from a sheaf on the For Sale sign. "Three bedrooms, two baths, eighteen hundred and seventy square feet," she says, climbing back into the car.

"Is there a pool?"

"No."

"Let me think," Sib says. "Sixty-two thousand."

"You win, Mom. Sixty-*four* thousand."

On the few miles home to Altadena, the silence between the two starts to thrum. Sib is about at the limit of what she can take of the girl. Those big eyes exaggerated by her glasses are so woozy and beseeching, they make Sib shrink back. Sib knows—they both know—that this is the time for her to check in, to ask how her daughter's doing. But Sib can't; she won't, she doesn't have it in her, whatever *it* is. She's all but holding her breath until they can go their separate ways. With both her girls now, she's at a loss. Sally, so odd and plain, gets too close, and Katie pushes Sib away. Sib loves them, she does, too much, and yet alone with either one, she wants to hide behind a stone wall.

"Aren't we getting milk?" Sally says.

Sib has lost track and passed the drive-through dairy, their usual last stop.

"I'll send Dad out later," she says. "I've got to get back. I have a lot of work to do." Really, another minute in this car and she'll explode. She needs her Hawaiian Punch. With a thimble-sized spike. Or, since it's Saturday, a two-thimble spike before tea later at Mrs. Wright's. "And please don't whine, Sally," she says.

"I wasn't whining. I just asked—"

"Well, you're whining now, so cut it out, okay?"

The girl turns away from her and looks out the passenger-side window. At the nape of her neck is a big rat's nest where her hair has rubbed against her collar.

"You know, Sal, if you can't keep your hair combed," Sib says, "we'll have to cut it short again."

"Mom!" Sally calls out, but she is crying, so it comes out, *Mob!*

"Oh for god's sake," Sib says, but that is all she says, because she, too, has begun to weep.

Because she began teaching late in November, Christmas comes fast. Sib has barely learned the names of her students and it is all carol singing and art projects—the sheaves of red and green construction paper the kids go through!—and rehearsals for the Christmas play, the Christmas concert, the pantomime.

Sib makes a blue-and-white bulletin board with a golden menorah for Hanukkah.

Not until Christmas vacation starts does she rally her courage and phone her former child-psychology professor. He sent a condolence card last summer, and on it he'd written his home number with *Call me anytime* underlined twice. She was too shy to call on her own behalf—this professor is a big personality and famous; his nickname is Dr. Love, sometimes he's on TV telling people to hug each other—she knew that the kindness in his voice would break her down. But she can call about a work matter, about Sandro. First, though, she has to go into Ellis's room to find the card. It's in a shoebox full of condolence cards that she shoved under the bed.

Phil thinks she hasn't cleared out Ellis's room because she can't bear to part with all the stuff. Really, it's the opposite. She wants it all gone, yesterday, without ever having to look at it again. She long ago took the things she wants: his Little League mitt, a boy-size cap, his near-bald teddy, plus a few bits the baby might like down the line—wooden building blocks, his high school ring (though he hadn't bothered to take it to college). She's saved, too, the high school yearbooks, where Ellis is pictured on the baseball and tennis teams, in the math club, and in the marching band. She'll let Socorro take what she wants for her family in Sinaloa, and the rest can go to Goodwill. Soon, time will force them to clear out the room, paint, buy the crib and the changing table.

No need to go overboard on the prep. Newborns need so little at the start. After three kids, Sib knows what's ahead—the changing, the feeding, the rocking, the bathing, the sleepless nights . . . and that's if all goes well. Even the best-case scenario—healthy, easy baby—frightens her now. So Sib trains herself not to think of the future, and she puts off what needs to be done to get there.

If only they could move. Start fresh: a new kid in a new house.

She finds her professor's card in the box; even his handwriting is outsize. She takes it into the kitchen.

"Oh, Sibyl." His voice is soft and thick with concern. "How are you doing, my friend?"

"You know," she says. "About as well as can be expected. I'm glad to be back at work. And thank you for writing; it meant a lot to get your note. But today I'm calling about a student. One of my fourth-grade boys."

She fills him in on Sandro's silence, his years in special ed, his high IQ. His mother's indifference.

There is a pause.

"Did you know I was in special ed as a kid?" her former professor says. "Same deal. When I was three, our family moved to Italy for a few years, and when we came back to California, my English was a shambles. The school put me in special ed and the so-called normal kids made fun of me. But my teacher was patient, very kind, and bit by bit, she straightened out my English. So I'd say, with your student, go slow. Be gentle."

Does everyone think she's pushy? "So far, I've just been observing him."

"Good. And since he's been mute for so long now, he's probably afraid that if he does speak, people will make a big deal of it. Keep it very low-key. Talk to him as if he's any other student. And don't let the other kids answer for him. Give him every opportunity to respond to you in a normal way. Be patient and kind and I promise . . ."

You'll never believe it," Sib says at the dinner table. Katie's eating at home for once, so they are four. "Over Christmas vacation my little math savant finished half the fifth-grade math book on his own. He taught himself base ten and decimals—and did about ten weeks' worth of problems."

"That's amazing, sweetheart," says Phil.

"Now, if only I can get him to stop chewing his pencils."

"Yeah, or maybe he'll die of lead poisoning," says Katie.

Sib goes to the ed center library after school and looks up what workbooks could supplement the usual math text. Then, she has an idea.

At their next tutoring session, she says, "Freddy, can I ask a favor? You know how Sandro's always alone at lunch and recess? I was wondering if you might make friends with him."

"I don't know, Mrs. Sam," says Freddy. "He might not go for it."

"Could you try? Maybe eat lunch with him. He probably won't answer but talk to him like he's any other kid. Be your usual friendly, cheerful self. Maybe walk home with him if he lives your way."

"What if he doesn't want to be my friend?"

Freddy, Freddy, she wants to cry out. *Anybody in their right mind would love to be your friend!* "It's worth a try. Please? As a favor to me?"

"Okay, Mrs. Sam."

Not a week later, Sib has a dentist appointment right after school gets out. A block away from Whitman, she passes Sandro and Freddy walking side by side down Fillmore Street. Freddy's hands are moving, and he's chattering away, and Sandro, well, Sandro is paying attention.

Oh god. Katie is at the piano. Those halting arpeggios. The girl doesn't know how to practice; when she makes a mistake, she either forges ahead or goes back to the very beginning instead of mastering the passage that tripped her. Sibyl can't say anything because these days Katie is a tinderbox. One word and she explodes.

The looks Katie gives her: it's as if she sees through to Sib's soul and finds it contemptible.

Sib never has got on her kids about practicing—or doing schoolwork, either. She won't do to her kids what her parents did to her. (On hearing that Sib had talent, her father soundproofed the basement and got her up at five every morning to practice the cello for two hours before breakfast.) Without her input, Ellis learned the clarinet in a snap and played it with a swagger; he had straight As, too. Katie also is a self-motivated A student, and diligent with the piano, though she has no ear. God, her latest recital piece, Chopin's Ashkenazi Waltz, she bashed out like a dancehall number.

Sally is the anomaly, all As and Ds—despite a soaring IQ, higher even than Ellis's was. But Sally won't do a thing that doesn't interest her, and only art and reading do, and reading barely.

Under cover of those stumbling arpeggios, Sib slips into the house, pees, fixes a Hawaiian Punch, and leashes Hinky. Dog and drink in hand, she heads out for a walk.

On the weekends—not every weekend—she and Phil try to do something with the girls. They drive to the snow and walk around, throw a few snowballs at each other, eat hamburgers on the way home. At the county art museum, Katie, bored and offended by the paintings, leaves a fauvist exhibit to sit outside. At *The Barber of Seville*, Sally whines to go home at intermission—although after the show, she is happy enough to eat a lamb French dip sandwich at Philippe's. Phil wants to go camping, but Katie has announced that she's never sleeping in a tent again and Sib quails at the prospect of so many hours in close quarters. Most of the time, they stay home and keep out of each other's way.

At her desk, with the math book open to quotients, Freddy softly says, "Mrs. Sam, I did like you said and just kept asking questions and pretending not to notice that he never answered, and the other day, when we were walking home from school, I said, 'Your house first or mine?' 'cause they're different ways to go, and he said, 'Yours.' And like you said to, I acted like nothing happened. I didn't tell you because what if that's the only time he ever talked? Then, yesterday we were eating lunch in the pergola, and I asked if he wanted chips and he said, 'Okay,' and again, I didn't act surprised, and today, without me saying anything first, he asked if I was going in—meaning was I coming in here or having lunch with him."

"And this was here at school?"

"I was thinking, Mrs. Sam, if he could come in here with us, he could eat his lunch while we do math. And you know how sometimes we just talk about stuff? Maybe he'll talk then too."

So now, Sandro is in his usual classroom seat, eating his lunch and reading a book while she and Freddy divide fractions by fractions. Sib says, "If we're too loud for you, Sandro, feel free to move farther back, it won't hurt our feelings." He nods and goes back to his book.

He nodded! She doesn't dare look at Freddy.

When he finishes eating, Sandro gets up and studies the guinea pig, a calico named Judy.

"Go ahead, take her out," Sib says.

Sandro holds the pig up to his face. Their noses twitch at each other.

Just before the bell, Freddy elbows her. Sandro is murmuring to Judy.

Sib parks in the driveway. The sun is sinking fast. It's March; the days are getting longer. She's pretty late. But Phil isn't home yet. So . . . just a quick walk around the block. She heads north, past the Romeros' house and the vacant lot behind it with the screen of five messy eucalyptus trees. In the Santa Ana winds, the trees bend and touch the top of the Romeros' house, and everyone—except the oblivious Romeros—worries that one day, one or all the trees will snap and crush the house. Sib turns the corner and is breathing in the trees' mentholated scent when she sees Sally on the ground next to the middle tree. Hunched over in her striped T-shirt and red corduroys, her hair in straggles, she looks tiny and gnomish beside the shaggy, thick trunk. She used to play here for hours with Ramona Romero, but Ramona is three years older and has started junior high at a new school and has new friends. Sally has been forgotten.

Sib can't bear it, really, to see Sally alone here in the dusk. She comes up quietly, close enough to see Sally's presiding over a small cluster of tiny, crude bark sheds arranged around a small street. The street is lined with little rocks, and the paths to each dwelling with thin, curving sticks. It's a miniature, ramshackle neighborhood.

"Oh, Sally Rose." Sib comes around so Sally can see her. "Come here, sweetie." She reaches down and grabs her daughter under her arms and pulls her to standing. Sib hugs her tightly, leans down to kiss her smelly stringy hair, again and again. Sally squirms finally and Sib releases her, steps back.

"Look, Mom," Sally says. Sibyl has inadvertently scattered one whole side of the little village. "And I just got it all back together."

The girls and Phil have now taken all they want from Ellis's room. Phil took only a pitching trophy and placed it on a bookshelf in the living room. One of the smaller, more tasteful of Ellis's prizes—a pitcher leaning back, front foot lifted, right hand cocked, about to let the ball fly—it's still that garish gold plastic on a fake wood base. But what can Sib say if Phil wants it on display?

Socorro packs up the rest of Ellis's stuff, taking one of three black garbage bags of clothes. Books, toys, trophies, pennants, prize ribbons go in boxes. The next morning, Sib calls St. Vincent de Paul. Phil sets everything out on the curb. When she comes home from work, the bags and boxes are gone.

She drives around the corner to the oleander hedge and howls into her arms.

Sib lifts her tumbler of Hawaiian Punch with its extra celebratory thimblefuls. Katie is again home for dinner. "Guess who answered a question in class today. Guess who named the capital of Oregon."

"Oh, sweetie, congratulations."

"And the other students were so good. You could see on their faces they were astounded—we all were—but we kept going as if nothing had happened."

"That's marvelous," says Phil. "Good for you."

"And it only took four months. Of course, I don't expect whole sentences yet, or actual conversation. Maybe by the end of the year. At recess I went in and told Mrs. Wright. She said bravo, and I deserved all the credit, but I probably shouldn't say anything in the faculty room, as it's the sort of thing that can make the other teachers feel inadequate. So I didn't say anything. But they should feel inadequate! Sandro had three other teachers before me—three!—and not one took the time to draw him out. Well, they'll know soon enough. Word gets around. Their unreachable elective mute is talking. And no thanks to them."

Sally's face is inches above her plate. She's shoveling in her salad. Katie's eyes are downcast, her ears are back. Only Phil is smiling and nodding at her. "That's wonderful, dear. Yes, best not to rile your colleagues."

Freddy, by April, is well into the sixth-grade math book. And Sandro is answering questions regularly, if tersely—in monosyllables mostly. He has yet to raise his hand or speak without being spoken to, though Freddy reports he's become quite the jabber-mouth with him. "Can I tell him to shut up now? Is that okay? To shut up and let me talk for a change?"

It takes her a moment to realize Freddy's joking. Mostly joking.

Phil found painters through a friend at work, and Ellis's yellow room is now a soft white. Still, Sib can barely think about the baby. She ran to Sears after work one day and ordered a new bassinet, a white crib and a matching changing table, which will come in a few weeks. Sally has been painting pictures to hang on the baby's walls: flowers, butterflies, birds. The closet drawers are already filled with diapers and onesies and receiving blankets thanks to Mrs. Wright, who gave Sib a baby shower one Saturday morning in her gracious, shaded backyard. The teachers went in on a fancy British-made baby carriage, with springs and a brake: an absurd contraption that Sib loves, though it seems designed more for walks in a large city park than the streets of west Altadena, which rarely have curbs, let alone sidewalks. Other friends contributed baby clothes, bottles, a diaper service, fuzzy toys.

When the new bassinet comes, Sib parks it next to her side of the bed, where one sat for each of her kids. Still, this baby is an abstract idea, one her mind can't fasten on for long. She'll believe it when she sees it. When the hot little bundle is placed in her arms.

So much could go wrong between now and then. The mother changing her mind. A problem with the birth. The other grandmother laying claim.

One afternoon, after a long day of teaching, Sib goes to read in her bedroom, Hawaiian Punch in hand, and finds Hinky asleep in the bassinet: she's wearing a onesie with daisies on it and tiny knit booties, pink on her front paws, baby blue on her back.

The call comes at three in the morning on the sixth of May. Labor's in full swing at the Oakland Kaiser. The baby carrier is already in the back seat of the Toyota. They have two totes of baby clothes and supplies all packed, and remembering that the Bay Area is chilly all year, they throw in jackets. Sib wakes up Katie. "Katie, hon, we're off. The baby's on its way. Socorro will come in the morning."

Next, she wakes Sally. "We're off to get the baby. Katie's here."

Sib phones the school district's messenger service to order a substitute teacher. She's brewing coffee for the thermos when Sally pads barefoot into the kitchen. She's fully dressed except for her white strappy sandals, which hang from one hand. Her corduroys, Sib sees, are inches too short. "I'm going to come."

"Oh, sweetheart. They won't let you in the hospital room. We couldn't leave you alone in the waiting room for god knows how long. And you have school."

"I should come. Or on the way home the baby will be all alone in the back seat."

Katie, in jeans and a pink T-shirt, comes in behind Sally. "I'm coming too."

"You girls need to be in school. And there's not enough room with the baby carrier in the back."

"So let's take the van."

"Phil," says Sib. He has walked into the kitchen. "The girls want to come."

"Fantastic," he says. "I'll move everything into the VW."

On the 5 through the Grapevine, they are in corridors of trucks, a sardine in a school of whales. Nobody talks. The old VW engine is too loud for conversation between the seats. Katie is in the middle. Sally is in her usual place in the far back, holding Hinky, who has already twice hopped into the baby carrier.

The sky out here is full of stars, powdered with stars.

Of course, Sib's thinking about the last time they drove up north together, when they went to fetch Ellis from that scruffy commune.

An hour on, the sky has paled. Rows of fruit trees stripe the low, rolling hills. *Imagine*, Sib thinks: *I'm forty-one years old, about to be a grandmother.* If this child—Ellis's child—is a boy, which she hopes, he will break her heart for how much—or how little—he is like his dad. If she's a girl, well, with girls she's . . . inadequate; their expectations, their needs seem fathomless. . . . Oh god. Sib gives herself a shake. It's just a thousand times easier to be a teacher than a parent! Just thinking of Freddy makes her smile, and Sandro—he only needed patient, steady encouragement. Teachers! Teachers are professionals, and parents are hopeless; they're amateurs, prone to mistakes, mistakes that can prove fatal.

She agreed to take this child many months ago. Now the time is here.

The stars have faded except for brightly gleaming planets. Sib turns to look at her daughters, who've also had a terrible year. She's been useless to them. Left them to themselves. Yet, surprisingly, here they are. Katie is curled up on the bench seat, asleep. Sally is gazing out the window and holding Hinky upturned like a baby. Sally's hair is a stringy mess. She catches Sib looking at her and brightens with excitement: *The baby is coming, and they're on their way to fetch it!* Using Hinky's paw, Sally waves. *Hi, Mom.*

In the slow noisy VW bus, in the dwindling darkness, accosted by her daughter's shining face, Sib allows herself a first small pulse of hope. She waves back. *Hi, darling.*

Fresh Water in the Sea

She was in Ojai checking out a boarding school for her younger son when a man near her said her name. "Yvette?" He had short, curly salt-and-pepper hair, a good tan, and kind brown eyes. Her body recognized him first: Phil Samuelson, fifteen years older. A person she'd never expected to see again.

Age had had its way with her as well, although her hair remained dark brown with only a few stray wires of white, and somehow (well, mostly by eating nothing) she was still slim, though with a tendency—and here is where age showed itself—to look fragile or, as her husband complained, skeletal.

"Is it really you?" she said, and, smiling, they embraced.

"You're not here for François," he said. "Surely he's, what . . ."

"A freshman at UCLA. I saw him yesterday. No. I'm here for my younger boy, JP. Jean Pierre."

"You and Claude got your two!"

"Yes. And you? Did you and"—here, somehow, from a deep drawer of memory, she extracted a name—"Sibyl—" She was about to say, "have another," but just then, the guide called the group to order and led them into the main building, which looked like a Spanish mission with its belfry.

Swamped by memories and long-ago feelings, Yvette worked to pay attention to the woman's recitation of school policies. Whenever she turned Phil's way, they smiled at each other, incredulous.

They toured classrooms; she'd read up on the architect, Austen Pierpont, who'd designed the auditorium with its all-glass back wall looking out on the Ojai Valley's citrus groves and the dining hall with its glass windows framing another view of terraced hillsides and marrow-colored mountains. The campus spanned several hundred acres; walking place to place gave them time for their present selves to eclipse their younger selves, so they became just who they were again, and familiar to each other.

The last time she'd heard from Phil was a note, thanking her for a condolence letter she'd sent after his son died. "It's the worst thing to happen in my life," he'd written.

Had she answered him? Probably. Probably with something inadequate, because what wouldn't be?

Early November gave them a pulsing blue sky and a cool breeze snaking up from the ocean. In the stables, horses stamped in their stalls: Thacher assigned every freshman a horse, which was why JP wanted her to check it out. Phil touched her arm. "Are you rushing off?" he said. "Or can we have lunch somewhere?"

She was staying at the Ojai Valley Inn—extravagant and ridiculously expensive, an indulgence—and didn't know any other place to go. He agreed to meet her there, at the inn's restaurant.

Clutching their folders of application forms and school pamphlets, they walked together to the parking lot. "You're not still in Saudi?" he said.

"That hateful place! We've been all over the world since: Bangkok, Jakarta, Madrid. We've landed in Oaxaca—Claude's retired."

"I always wondered," Phil said.

She knew what he wondered: if her marriage had lasted.

Had his? So many marriages don't survive the death of a child.

They reached her rental car first, and she sat in its sun-warmed interior for some minutes before turning the key.

She'd married Claude twenty-two years ago against the advice of her older sister, Marie Claire, who'd said, "He's too old!" (Yvette was twenty-seven, Claude forty-eight.) "He is not handsome," Marie Claire had continued. "You'll have ugly babies with his nose. Right now, you think you love him because he's the big man at your job. But he's stealing the last of your most beautiful years!"

Yvette had thought Claude quite handsome, in particular his nose, which was like a big wedge of granite, formidable and sexy. More to the point—and she couldn't make this clear to Marie Claire—working with him was the most potent attractor. Here she was, fresh out of Yale architecture school, a mere intern at his firm, and he'd tapped her to do his lettering, and then to discuss and draft his ideas, and draft and draft and draft them until she was channeling—and shading, then revising—his vision. He roared his approval. He improved on her improvements and she on his. The clock hands spun; more than once they worked through till dawn, the floor covered with curls of flimsy. She could not quite convey this to Marie Claire, but working like that was as intimate as sex. No, *more.*

Marie Claire had come to Boston from Baltimore to meet Claude—there was an uncomfortable dinner at the Charles Hotel—and to give Yvette a wedding shower.

She'd booked a back room at a ladies' lunch restaurant. Their mother, who was in Panama with her new husband, couldn't come, but Yvette's two friends from Claude's firm did, along with former classmates from New York and New Haven, and her roommate from Emma Willard, her old boarding school. One of Claude's two daughters showed up as well, nineteen-year-old Nonie. (Twenty-one-year-old Charlotte was at Bowdoin.)

Yvette had stipulated no household gifts because she and Claude were moving overseas. The women from the firm gave her naughty lingerie, which embarrassed her in front of Nonie, but Nonie laughed with everyone else at the fishnet, the nipple holes and crotch snaps. As soon as everyone left, Yvette wound all that obscene frippery into a ball and tossed it into the dumpster out back.

They married at the courthouse the next day, Marie Claire and Nonie their witnesses.

Marie Claire gave her a copy of *Middlemarch*, which, although heavy, Yvette took on the plane, a twenty-four-hour flight. She read it too, or enough to know why Marie Claire had given it to her.

But Claude was not at all like Mr. Casaubon; he was not a withered, celibate old bachelor pedant. Claude's legs were strong and admirable. He'd been married before, for twenty years, and divorced for four. Her friends at his firm said he'd gone through some postdivorce craziness, sleeping with every woman he could. But then, they added, in laughing whispers, he'd done that in his marriage, too, so no big surprise, the divorce. "Watch out," they'd told her when she was new. "Sex is Claude's way of shaking hands."

To Yvette, Claude was more like literature's reformable rakes, a Mr. Rochester or Fred Vincy: a large man, a little overweight maybe, with faded red curls spilling over his forehead, a bowtie ever askew. Without a wife to tell him when to cut his hair or to tuck in his shirt, he was a shambles. A big, sexy shambles.

From the start, he tried; he asked her out for lunch, for drinks, for dinner. He touched her lower back as she drew. He said she had the best drafting hand in the business. "Your lettering is flawless, very professional, yet somehow amusing," he said. "Almost antic in style . . ." He put her on his biggest project, a corporate center in Guinea with an extravagant budget. ("Aluminum money," he said.) She played innocent, impervious to his hangdog looks and sulks, and mimed surprise when he stormed off in a huff for no obvious reason—he had quite the repertoire. She refused to join his long list of easy conquests. Even after she fell in love with him and thought about him nonstop, and now yearned for the brush of his arm, the proprietary nudge, she resisted, and with increased rigor. Pride. When she understood that he'd be moving to Conakry to supervise the construction of their complex, she spent a night thrashing in her bed.

He was leaving in a month.

They were working late in an empty office when Claude stood back from the table and said, "Okay, I get it. You're a serious girl. So what is it you want? A husband? Is there any chance for me? What great tasks must I perform to qualify?"

She had thought this through ten thousand times and had an answer ready: "You must be willing to have at least two more children. You must stop with the women. We must keep working together. And travel. I want to live in the world."

"Is that all?" he said, and slid his arms around her. "Then I think you will like Conakry. There are many French people there."

She had grown up in Lyon with an American mother and a Lyonnaise father. After her father died—she was fourteen—

she'd lived first in London, then in the States for boarding school, college, and work up till now.

To accompany Claude to Guinea, she put off getting her architect's license. No problem, for didn't she now have work for life?

Yvette did enjoy the two years they spent in Conakry. She was on the payroll along with Claude, she spoke French almost exclusively, and she learned how to cook.

Africa only whetted her interest in international life. After Conakry, Claude took a contract to design and build a skyscraper in Al Khobar, Saudi Arabia. She assumed they'd work together there, too; Claude said of course, but this time unofficially. They had their own team. Who's they? she asked. Parsons, the engineering firm who'd hired him. Were his team members Saudi? No, just some men in their Saudi offices. *Men.* Men with licenses? Not necessarily. Just *men.*

She got pregnant their first month in Dhahran. François was named for her father, and for a while he kept her so busy she forgot she was an architect or even a separate being; she almost forgot she was in Saudi. This was in 1970 and they lived in Aramco's Dhahran American camp, a bubble—or as she called it, a snowless globe—of American clichés. She spent her days with her son and a tall, white-blond friend named Astrid, another young mother. Astrid and her husband, a petrochemical engineer, were from Denmark and had already lived in the camp for five years. Astrid painted and read novels, which she and Yvette discussed while pushing strollers through the compound's swooping roads to the pools and parks, the stable and stores where they observed with mixed amusement and disbelief as the other young mothers, many of whom were from Texas and Oklahoma, reenacted American suburban life without a trace of irony: here were Boy Scouts, Girl Scouts, Little League, barbecues, casseroles, the Easter Bunny, Santa, jack-o'-lanterns, mistletoe. The international workers—from India, Europe, South America—were still a minority, although now the only requirement for admission was a Western lifestyle. Aramco residents drank. The women drove cars (only in the camp) and wore sleeveless tops and dresses, and, according to Astrid, slept around (punishable by death outside the compound, supposedly).

Enclosed by fences and razor wire, they lived in low-slung ranch-style houses, some stuccoed, some clapboard, with front and back yards, picture windows, front porches. The houses were remodeled to order for each new tenant, though the construction values in Yvette and Claude's "executive level" three-bedroom were not what they expected, with the drapes woven of some shiny extruded yarn, the kitchen cabinetry shoddy. The wall-to-wall carpet crunched like straw when walked on. *Crunch, crunch.*

Shocked by the ugliness, they'd quickly looked at rentals in the nearby city of Al Khobar, where the Saudis lived behind high thick walls in rooms centered on interior courtyards—an inversion of the camp's sprawling openness. Yvette would be isolated enough with an infant, she decided, and with Claude gone so much, she couldn't give up Astrid, the pools, and the parks.

She ordered expensive wool carpet and custom-made cabinets, which took almost a year to arrive. In the meantime, she found it remarkable what even a finicky person like her could get used to: *crunch crunch crunch.*

They had been in Saudi almost four years—the region was settling down after the Yom Kippur War and oil embargo—and Astrid had been gone for two years, when word came that a new project supervisor was coming to replace the man Claude had always worked with. The timing couldn't be worse for a new man to jump in, Claude said, as he was in the home stretch of his latest—and, Yvette hoped, his last—Saudi project, the upgraded Dhahran air terminal. The new supe would have a lot of catching up to do.

"Phil Samuelson? We met him in Pasadena," Irv Matthews said at that night's buffet dinner. "Terrific guy. Though Jewish, I think."

"If he is, they might not let him in," said Claude.

Jews supposedly were not allowed into Saudi, especially now, after the war.

Ruth Matthews said, "Oh, Phil's lovely. His wife, though, is a prickly thing. But isn't that always the case: the easygoing marry the prickles because who else would have them? I heard they offered him a much bigger job if he'd move here with his family, but she put her foot down."

Yvette wished she'd put her foot down. Her dusty little Belgian pump.

She also wondered who, in her marriage, was the prickly one. Claude had his moods and his temper. But she was the snob, the complainer.

"Anyway, when you meet Phil, you'll see," said Ruth. "A real sweetheart."

A few weeks ago, Yvette had come upon Ruth Matthews kissing Arvin Schrader in the Ealings' back bathroom. Was poor Phil Samuelson Ruth's next-in-line?

They were all sick of each other and starved for new blood.

There was a buffet dinner at someone's house most nights. The host grilled meat; women brought side dishes. They'd feed the kids first, stick them in a bedroom with toys and a TV, then get down to drinking and eating and telling the same old stories. Claude and three-year-old François enjoyed these gatherings; Yvette had never gotten comfortable with the easy racism and conservatism, the Wonder bread and canned string beans, the lack of curiosity about the world outside.

Still. What else was there to do?

Bob and Laura Taylor hosted on a Sunday, their buffet

indistinguishable from all the others: the eternal bathtub booze, freezer-burned meat, and two-ton casseroles. The Matthewses came in with the new supervisor and introduced him around. Phil Samuelson was another pale American engineer of average height, average looks, with a short, rippled frizz of light brown hair. Not anyone Yvette would've looked at twice.

Ruth Matthews filled a plate for him, which he ate standing with the men clustered around the bottles in the dining room. His white sport shirt was too starched, too bright, and too large in the shoulders, which made him look slumped. The prickly wife, Yvette thought, should have attended to that.

The women colonized the living room, where the talk was of children and the massive new Safeway in Al Khobar. "You can buy a refrigerator there. And lipstick!"

"May I?" Phil appeared at the far end of Yvette's sofa. "I'm bushed." He set his drink on the coffee table and sat. The women volleyed questions at him: how many kids (three), how old (seventeen, fourteen, and eight), how long was he staying (the usual two weeks), was this his first time in Saudi (to Dhahran, but he'd been in Jeddah a lot). And what was the news back home—just how high were gas prices?

"Over fifty cents a gallon," said Phil.

Shrieks. *You're joking!*

"Nope. Filled my car up two days ago."

He had an amusing way of turning toward whoever was

speaking—he swung his head with a little swoop—as if each speaker snagged his attention in turn.

François wandered in, stretched out in between them, and fell asleep with his head on Yvette's lap and his toes pressing into Phil's thigh. Phil shook his ankle affectionately. A dad.

From their sofa, Yvette and Phil had a clear view into the dining room, where the men were getting loud and red-faced. Claude was his big, boisterous, boozed-up self, roaring with laughter at the other men's stories, thumping their backs, topping off their drinks. His hair had gone whiter in the past six years, but it still tumbled over his forehead like a bull's. He was a great favorite with this Aramco crowd. They found him elegant, *plus raffiné*.

A sudden outcry of wails and screams issued from the kids' room; the other mothers rose as one and rushed down the hall. Yvette stayed, pinned to the sofa by François.

"I'm going to sneak out now," Phil said, standing. "I'm gooey with jet lag."

"I'd go too, but this one"—she touched her son's curls—"needs to be carried. And that one"—she nodded to Claude—"has some life in him yet."

"I'll take him, if you like," Phil said, wagging François's foot. "That way, I can see where you live. I'm meeting Claude there in the morning."

She went to Claude and told him their plan. "Unless you're ready to go."

"I'll come in a bit," he said, as she knew he would.

They walked down the wide quiet streets with François draped over Phil's shoulder like a lion skin. It was May and the air still rang from the day's heat. The stars formed a bright loose cloud overhead. "So. Welcome to Aramco Dhahran," said Yvette. "Or as we call it, 'the Magic Kingdom.'"

"You can't fool me. I might have flown for fifty hours, but this is the San Fernando Valley. And not its prettiest subdivision, either."

"I know. It's awful."

"It didn't have to be," Phil said. "I worked with an architect, Gregory Ain—"

"Oh, he's great."

"—who designed some small modernist subdivisions—"

"Yes—the Park Planned Homes, the Avenel Housing projects."

"So you know! Aramco should have hired him."

"Or someone! Even I could design a more beautiful development."

"You're an architect?"

"All but the license."

"Like me," said Phil. He'd studied with Ain, and worked on Ain's last few projects, he said, then designed and built his own modernist home. He'd started classes for an architecture degree, but life intervened: marriage, kids, well-paying jobs. "Then extremely well-paying jobs," he said. "Which is why I'm here."

"Parsons won't hire me. Women can't work here in any professional capacity. Only as file clerks and typists. And Parsons goes along with it."

"The dirtbags," he said.

"Exactly," she said.

He had a low trill of a laugh.

He carried François all the way to his bed and refused a cup of coffee—"I need a good thirty hours of sleep!"—and left, shutting the front door so softly, Yvette wasn't sure he'd gone.

She liked him. So quiet and gentle and easy to talk to. So un-Claude.

Claude swam laps every morning and was at the pool when the call came that he was wanted in Jeddah. A car was coming to take him to the airport. Yvette got his suit and shoes ready. This was not the first time he'd been summoned to Saudi's west coast at the last minute; one of the lead architects on the new airport there had fallen ill, and Claude would stand in for him at key meetings.

The car took Claude away. Yvette walked François to his nursery school and when she got home, Phil Samuelson was standing on her porch. In the last-minute scramble, Claude had forgotten to call him.

"I'll take that cup of coffee, now," said Phil. He didn't have another appointment till noon.

It was ninety-four degrees out at nine in the morning. She'd thrown on a blue spaghetti-strap dress she'd bought in Saint-Tropez last year, an expensive scrap of beachwear. As she led him inside, she felt self-conscious, underdressed, with too much skin on display.

Earlier, Claude had spread some drawings on the coffee table, so Phil was looking these over while she made coffee. She slipped into the bedroom and put on a light cotton sweater—then took it off. Even with air-conditioning it was too hot.

When she brought the coffee in to him, Phil was asleep on the sofa.

She set the cups down and sat a cushion away. He slept silently. Claude was never so quiet; even in sleep he rattled and snored and wheezed and heaved about.

Phil had on another fresh white short-sleeved shirt, also too big, too starched, and creased from folding. But his arms were nicely shaped, with wide wrists and large, square hands. "Hey." She touched his forearm. "Coffee's here."

He caught her hand and held it tightly against his thigh.

"Phil," she said, and tried, gently, to take her hand back. He tightened his grip and gave a little snore. His eyes fluttered and stilled. Clearly, he was asleep again—if he'd ever been awake.

Even if he wasn't asleep, his clasp seemed neither flirtatious nor assaultive, but more like how you'd hold the hand of someone injured or grieving. Though which one suffered and which one comforted here was up for grabs.

She and Claude had never planned to be in Saudi so long, but Parsons kept offering Claude big projects with full creative control, and the money—the *deluge* of money—was hard to refuse. Many wives found ways to spend that money—that was one occupation they were allowed—shopping: ordering items from the States, seeking out rugs and antiques in the bazaars, going on buying trips to Paris and Rome. Some wives used the camp like a live-in country club, playing tennis or riding horses in the cool mornings with bridge games and maybe swimming until the schools discharged their children. Very few of them missed working the way Yvette did. She tried to busy herself; she taught a French class and made dishes for the buffet dinners, a minor competitive sport in which she ranked low, losing to what Astrid had called the Cream o' Mushroom Soup Set.

Parsons allotted their employees two lifesaving eight-week vacations a year; she and Claude and François went to Gstaad and skied in the winter; in the summer, they rented a beach house near Fréjus on the Mediterranean, where Claude's daughters joined them. Twice, taking François, Yvette had met Marie Claire in Lyon at Easter. She'd tried to go again this year but was refused an exit visa—after the oil embargo Saudi officials were making it harder for Westerners to come and go as they pleased.

When they'd moved here, in the smallest of their bedrooms, she'd set up a drafting table with a new Borco cover and Mayline straightedge, her pencils, triangles, sharpeners, and Rapidograph pens arranged on a side table. Claude threw her some lettering jobs at first, but she saw the final plans, and her work was never on them.

Now, since they had about a year left, she wanted to have her second baby. What else was there to do?

Phil Samuelson stirred and sighed. And squeezed her hand. Sweet.

Claude loved having a son; he tossed François in the air, jostled him on his knee, noisily blew raspberries on the boy's belly so that he howled with joy. But Claude had neither engaged with nor enjoyed the feeding, the diapering, the bathing, the nonstop tending. He'd grumbled and sulked at the drag on Yvette's attention, her ceaseless bustling, her exhaustion. Now, although he'd agreed to a second child, he was clearly not eager. Subtly, he avoided her, rushing off to swim first thing in the morning, coming late to bed, when she was already asleep. With the right mix of liquor and teasing, Yvette might jolly him into making love; more often he was too tired or too drunk, or had too much on his mind.

Phil Samuelson snored and woke himself up. "Oh, hello," he said, swinging his head her way. Seeing their hands, he immediately let go. "Goodness! Sorry! I was having the nicest dream. I dreamt I was holding my daughter Katie's hand, which she hasn't allowed in years! How embarrassing. I hope I didn't offend you."

Yvette said, "No, no. I could tell you were asleep, and I didn't want to wake you. The jet lag here is brutal."

"You're very kind."

"Katie must be your teenager."

"Bingo."

They moved to the kitchen and sat at the counter eating slices of cold watermelon.

"Your husband's in high demand. Going forward we have some great opportunities for him."

"The Dhahran terminal is his last project here," she said seditiously. Claude hadn't informed Parsons yet that they were done. "He promised me."

"Not the new Jeddah airport?"

"We've given Saudi enough of our lives," she said. "I don't want François growing up in this ersatz suburbia stuffed with bigots and surrounded by razor wire."

"Huh. Well. That changes things."

Reckless, she went on: "I heard your wife refused to live here."

"Yes, but our kids are older and in school—the boy's graduating this year. We couldn't dislodge them at this stage of their lives. Anyway, Sibyl—my wife—would never live in an Arab country."

"Ah," said Yvette. "So you are Jewish."

"I've been told not to wave it on a banner here, but yes."

At noon he called a car and went into Al Khobar for his next meeting.

She waved and closed the door, equally relieved and disappointed to find herself alone.

That night at the Brewers' buffet, Ruth Matthews and some other wives had Phil cornered in the living room. He saw Yvette come in and waved, raising his eyebrows in mock fright—*Look! I've been captured!*—then made no move to escape and join her. Claude hadn't come back from Jeddah yet, so she left before dessert, while François was awake and ambulatory. "Good night, everyone," she called. Phil swung his head her way with such verve, she expected him to jump up and walk them home.

He called good night from his chair.

How surprising, how sharp was her disappointment.

The next buffet was at the Schraders' midweek, and Yvette missed it to teach her French class. Her students were half a dozen eighth graders headed to boarding schools in Geneva and Provence—there were no secondary schools in Dhahran for Western kids. Leaving for high school was a rite of passage here. "Graduating," they called it.

She wished that she could graduate with them. Claude said the earliest they could leave was next April or May. A year.

She found Claude and Phil going over drawings in the living

room. "Phil's driving up the coast tomorrow for a look-see," Claude said. "I told him to take you. Do you good to get out and about."

Phil looked up to catch her response. She tried not to look too pleased.

She called the babysitter, who agreed to pick up François from school the next day and keep him till Yvette got home.

The Dammam Port was at the end of a seven-mile causeway in the Persian Gulf. Along the way, men were fishing and families picnicking by the water in the glinting late-morning sunlight. In other places, cranes and steel girders signaled the construction of new shipping docks. "In a year, you won't know the place," said Phil. "I've seen the expansion plans."

About halfway down the causeway, he pulled over. They got out and walked along the hard-packed sand. "I read that there's a freshwater spring out here—in the middle of the sea. People used to come in boats for fresh drinking water. With the new desalinization plants, they don't bother anymore."

"How did anybody find fresh water in a sea?"

"That's what I want to know. A change in color? An obvious current or bubbling?"

They walked maybe half a mile up one side and down the other, scanning the inscrutable blue-green water. Twice, her headscarf flew off in the stiff hot breeze and Phil chased it down. He held her arm over the rocks and pulled her back when, from the wake of a boat, the water surged toward her. "It's either too subtle to see, or we're in the wrong place," he said, and they got back in the car.

On the mainland again, in the small city of Qatif, they ambled along narrow streets where some of the older houses had beautiful wooden doors carved with fluid Arabic script. "Verses from the Koran would be my guess," said Phil.

"Blessings," said Yvette.

She had hardly been out of the Aramco compound this year, except to shop. Last winter, there had been a company boat trip in the gulf, and in March, a bus tour to the great Al Ahsa oasis, where she'd gotten more than eighty mosquito bites—she and Claude counted while daubing on the calamine—but they hadn't done a lazy daylong wander like this in months, maybe a year.

A much cruder, narrower stone-built causeway took them to the tiny island village of Darin, where they parked and browsed through a dusty stall selling clay jars, a few brass bowls, some well-used camel saddlebags. The owner brought out a crumpled paper sack and spilled pearls in whites, pinks, and yellows onto a dirty glass counter. Yvette liked a rope of irregular yellow ones that glowed gold at the edges. Phil picked out some large luminous whites for his wife and asked Yvette for help choosing some for his teenage daughter. Yvette untangled a double strand of pink seed pearls. "These."

"Beautiful, yes. I'll have to tell Katie you picked them out, because she'll never wear them if she thinks I did. She says my taste in clothes is a disaster."

Yvette stepped back and gave him a playful, appraising look. "You could try going one size down," she said.

He laughed his low trill, embarrassed, yet pleased to be teased.

He haggled briefly with the shopkeeper in Arabic, then paid for the pearls, including her yellow ones. He insisted she put them on and lowered them over her head himself.

"So pretty," he said.

They ate grilled fish in Al Jubail, a sleepy seaside village slated, Phil said, to become the world's largest industrial complex. New cinder-block construction was everywhere—new houses, new schools, a clinic. They heard booms through the restaurant's tall open windows and saw rising clouds of dust as old mud-brick structures were demolished.

They walked to the beach and down a jetty where fishermen were mending nets, pulling the ropy webs taut with their toes as they stitched up rips, their awls flying. Farther on, a man was building a cage of wire mesh large enough to hold a man or two. Finished cages were stacked nearby. Fish traps, Phil said, pointing out how a wire funnel allowed fish to enter, while its spokes made it virtually impossible for them to get out.

By late afternoon the heat had risen, and humidity thickened the air. This was a relentless country, she thought, the dusty monochromatic desert and towns, the flat blue-green gulf, this stifling wet heat. They drove and talked and were quiet and then talked some more.

"Why are you smiling?" he asked as they were coming into Al Khobar.

"Oh, nothing," she said. "Just how you turn your head whenever someone speaks. Like they've literally hooked your attention."

"Yeah. I should probably rein that in. I got it from our dog, Hinky. She tracks conversation from person to person with this perky little head swing. We've all imitated her so much it's become a family tic. I don't even know I'm doing it. I should cut it out."

"Oh, don't," said Yvette.

A message stuck in her screen door said that Claude would not be back from Jeddah until tomorrow night. She made martinis from his stash of good liquor; pure gin, an olive, icy cold.

"Finally," said Phil. "A decent drink. That bathtub rotgut could strip paint."

"Claude has a friend in the diplomatic corps. They don't have to go through customs. So the guy brings in booze by the suitcase-ful."

"Cheers!" Phil clinked her glass. "Will you really leave when Claude's finished the terminal?"

"The minute it's signed off," said Yvette.

"What if Parsons were to hire you? I could make a case for it," he said.

"Too late," she said. "I hate it here."

He flinched at her sharpness. Wasn't he used to prickliness?

"There are so many other places in the world to see," she said. "Places I can work. Saudi isn't good for women."

"You won't move back to the States?"

"For a while, maybe," she said. To see her sister and Claude's daughters. "But we like living abroad. Being footloose—with nowhere in particular we call home."

"I can't imagine that," he said. "No home. Don't you want one?"

"Not really." She took his glass and made new drinks. "I do miss having friends in my field, other architects and designers." The alcohol was forming a large, cold space where anything could be said. "Here, well, I have never been so bored in my life. I have Claude, of course, who's brilliant company"—she lowered her voice—"but he's so busy and gone so much, I hardly see him. And"—now she was half-whispering—"ever since François was born, he's lost interest. I mean, he hardly touches me."

"Oh," said Phil. "I see." And again came that whimsical swing of his head to look at her. His eyes were amused and kind. "Well, we can take care of that right now."

For the next eight days, they stole every half hour or half day they could, as Claude was back and forth to Jeddah, François at school or sleeping. They planned another field trip—this time to go down along the coast—for when Phil returned in July.

In June a letter came addressed to Yvette and Claude both. His son, Phil wrote, had gone on a camping trip and not come back. "He has called and written, so we know he's alive, but we still don't know where he is. I can't leave Sib and the girls at such a precarious time, so I've prepped my colleague Ed Hunt to do this supervision and hopefully I'll see you both in September."

At a buffet in August, the Matthewses came in saying, "Terrible, terrible news. You know Phil Samuelson? We just heard that his son drowned."

Yvette had cried out, pulled François close, and hidden her face in his neck until she caught her breath. She wrote to Phil the next day, sent her condolences. He replied, this time to her alone, "Thank you for writing, your words mean so much. We'd found our boy and brought him home for a week before he went off to college. Thank God we had that time with him because the day before his classes were to begin, he went swimming with friends, got caught in some submerged trees, and drowned. We are in a sorry state here in Altadena, and I can't see leaving Sib and the girls alone in the foreseeable future. Parsons has kindly given me an office job at headquarters. I'm sorry not to see you; it would've been a comfort. . . ."

That was the last she knew of Phil Samuelson.

She felt sad for him, for his loss, but she was not sad that he wasn't coming back. Claude had either sensed a rival or noticed a shift in her—a new self-containment or detachment—that reawakened his ardor: he didn't leave her alone for months. (Yvette later confided to Marie Claire that Phil had "sexed her up.") Their last year in Saudi saw a recommitment, a rekindling of their original connection that was welcome, fun, and fruitful. She and Claude left the following April, as soon as their second son, Jean Pierre, could travel.

A thousand times, Yvette had counted the weeks: JP, born 43.5 weeks after Phil Samuelson left the Aramco camp, was either a super-late post-term baby or, far more likely, Claude was the father.

At any rate, so far as she and everyone else was concerned, Claude was the father.

Through the years, in the long hours she spent watching her boys play in Boston's parks, then in Sanam Luang in Bangkok, Suropati Park in Jakarta; or waiting in the string of cars to drop them off and pick them up at schools, she'd recall the warm grip of Phil's hand, the comic swerve of his head, his fingers grazing her neck as he lowered the yellow pearls over her head; each moment a rung to the sweetness and good humor of their lovemaking. This was a private source of replenishment to her, like a secret garden, a spring of fresh water in the sea.

Phil was already seated at a table on the inn's patio.

"Sorry, I had a message at the desk to call home," she said.

"Big crisis. JP couldn't find his piano music—he'd left it in my car."

They ordered salads and gazed out across the valley, the tidy citrus groves, the red tiled roofs of the town, the dark, jagged mountains. The ocean breeze came in cool drafts.

She showed him the photos in her wallet: JP dark and slim like her; red-blond François with Claude's broad shoulders and rocklike nose.

She and Claude had moved back to Boston after Saudi, she told Phil. They bought a house in the South Bay, then left it for years at a time to work in Thailand, Indonesia, and Spain; the boys had turned out quite adventurous and adaptable. "After Claude retired, we moved to Oaxaca for a last family adventure—and so the boys could keep up their Spanish." They'd built a large home in a nearby village, San Felipe del Agua, and kept a smaller apartment in the Centro for work. "No more big international projects," Yvette said; now they mostly designed houses for expats, and the occasional restaurant or resort. "We can be as busy as we like. And you?"

"Still in Altadena, in my same old house. I left Parsons, and corporate life, to open a small company with a couple of other engineers—more or less a boutique firm for architects working on public projects. A lot of environmental remediation stuff."

"And your future Thacher student is . . . ?"

"Eva, if she gets in, and wants to go. My son, Ellis—who drowned—left a pregnant girlfriend. She couldn't take on a kid, so Sib and I adopted her. I know that all babies constellate love, but little Eva was really the loveliest, most droll child, so charming, so easy. She saved us, she really saw us through. Now, Sib's gone, too."

"No! I'm so sorry. . . ."

"Almost three years ago—breast cancer. A lump she ignored for years." He gave a listless wave of his hand, and Yvette took hold of it.

They sat quietly, holding hands in the old comforting way. They looked at each other until both began to smile their familiar, conspiratorial smiles. After all, they had the hotel—her room, at least—at their disposal. Phil squeezed her hand and then let go. "The thing is," he said, "I've asked my girlfriend to move in with me. She and Eva like each other, but neither is keen to share a house—and me, I suppose—with the other. Boarding school was Pam's idea, and Eva likes the sound of Thacher, especially the horses. But she's gotten into a great school in Pasadena which is probably where she should go. And just yesterday, her birth mom offered to take her for high school in Walnut Creek."

"She knows her birth mom?" Yvette picked up her fork and went back to her salad.

"They connected after Sib died. Which has been wonderful for Eva. Still, Walnut Creek's farther than I'd like to see her go, and she's never really liked it there. Thacher would be an easy weekend drive."

"I'm not keen to have JP so far away either," said Yvette. "But it was his idea, now that he's stuck at home with us old folks. Here, he'd be an hour from François. And I could visit both in one trip."

They smiled at each other, a little sadly now, through another comfortable silence, another current of cool ocean air.

"If it matters," said Yvette, "you were my only, ah, petite affaire."

"Likewise. Not something I ever expected of myself before or since."

She touched her neck. "I still wear the yellow pearls. All the time."

"Oh god—remember that guy with his rumpled paper sack? And out poured a treasure." Phil laughed his low trill. "Like a fairy tale."

Yvette stilled. That laugh: she recognized it, she knew it well—but not from him. She'd been hearing it for years now. The exact same low staccato chortle. Unmistakable.

Could it be? An enormous rearrangement began within.

She walked him to his car. "Let's keep in touch this time," he said.

"Yes and let me know if Eva chooses Thacher." Because if Eva was going to Thacher, she'd send JP somewhere, anywhere else.

Claude had already been through prostate cancer and triple bypass surgery. His doctor had forbidden him to drink, so he now drank only on weekends. He still roared and commanded attention and charmed women and men alike. Except for the years in Saudi, he'd given her a life of marvelous work, international travel, and a loving, rambunctious family. She would allow no rude, disruptive revelations in his last years. She'd protect him till the end.

And save Phil Samuelson for later.

All the Sounds of the Earth

The plane had taken off and when it leveled out, the back third of the cabin burst into song. *June is busting out all over!*

It was not June. It was March 1986, and below, in eastern Pennsylvania, no trees had leaves.

Katie Samuelson was in 20C, an aisle seat, and when the singing subsided to a low chant, the woman next to her said, "John Adams High School chorus. They just performed at Carnegie Hall."

"Wow." Katie was being polite. She disliked musicals. Whenever actors burst into song, she was embarrassed for them.

"Oh, anyone can sing at Carnegie," the woman said. "It's a pay-to-play thing. All last year the kids raised money to rent the stage, pay for the chorus leader, the plane fare, the costumes. Thank god it's over. Almost over."

They had to stop talking when singers hit the chorus again.

Katie hadn't slept in twenty-five hours. She'd just finished the last sixteen-hour shift of her general surgery rotation, then stayed on to help Gavin Yu, the intern, finish the scut work—the notes, reports, and medication orders. She'd dashed home, packed, and splurged on a cab to JFK.

She was reading *Mansfield Park*, or trying to. She'd been reading it since she began her ob-gyn rotation in October, then all through pediatrics and neurology. Now, after ten weeks of surgery, she was still only to chapter twelve. Every time she read a page, she dozed off.

The song ended, and she tried to return to poor Fanny, alone in mistrusting the devious Crawford siblings, but thoughts of Gavin intruded: his unexpected, clumsy embrace in the storeroom before she left.

Oh what a beautiful morning started softly in the back rows. One verse, two, and building. She resented and resisted a throb of nostalgia; her mother loved *Oklahoma!* and had played the record frequently, for years. *All the sounds of the earth are like music / All the sounds of the earth are like music* . . . Then the tenors really cut loose. Too much! All the aisle people glanced back, annoyed.

The steward went to the rear of the plane and said something, and there was no more singing.

Katie was flying home to California because her mother had metastatic breast cancer and was about to die. Last May, Sib had gone to the doctor with back pain. He ordered X-rays and that's how they found it. The cancer was already in her lymph nodes and spine.

Sib couldn't, or wouldn't, say how long since her last mammogram. "Two years, maybe three," she'd told Katie. "My breasts were always lumpy bumpy. Every mammo they'd call me back for a sonogram and every time, it was just benign cysts. So I skipped a mammo or two because it was always the same old rigmarole."

"But you know that early detection . . ." Katie was too irritated to finish a sentence. "And we're Ashkenazi, prone to . . ."

She didn't blame her mother for getting cancer, only for not attending to it.

Phil told Katie that, according to the doctor, Sib hadn't been screened for seven years.

Sib went through a round of chemo with all the resulting nausea, hair loss, fatigue, and neuropathy. But it slowed the cancer enough that she was able to go back to teaching last fall.

Katie was home for three days over the holidays and Sib was down to 102 pounds. Short, weirdly kinky gray hair had replaced her bowl cut of fine, mink-brown hair.

Sib went back to work after New Year's, but her principal sent her home at the first recess. The cancer had gone into her liver.

Katie's father and sisters urged Sib to do another round of chemo, but for what? Another month? And probably not a good month either. Anyway, Sib refused. "I'll just see it through," she said.

Last week, Phil had called Katie to say she had better come

home, that Sib now had hospice care and was near the end. Katie didn't see how she could go; her next rotation was starting right away. But she asked, and her supervisor said given the circumstances, she could make up the time later, in extra shifts.

She went mostly because she didn't want to have regrets down the line.

Katie knew that many, even most daughters—the good daughters—would take time off from school to nurse a sick mother. Her freshman college roommate had flown home when her mother had a facelift.

She and Sib weren't that kind of close. Or any other kind. Their connection was more a trembling hairlike wire that gave off intermittent system-wide shocks. Katie couldn't remember a time when she and her mother were easy with each other. She'd been a long-standing disappointment to Sib: plump until puberty ("I have to do something about Katie's weight!"); she had too much too curly hair ("I must get that hair of Katie's thinned again!"); Sib deemed her feet too flat for ballet ("Pity because that might've given her a little grace"). When Katie became tall and thin and pretty at twelve, Sib lamented that she was flat-chested ("Poor Katie has no figure").

As for her academic achievements? ("Ah, here's Katie, my overachiever.")

She learned to stay out of her mother's way. She practiced the piano before Sib got home from work so she wouldn't have to hear her remarks ("Is that a jackhammer at the keys?"). She kept to her room.

Sib had only ever really enjoyed and approved of Ellis. Ellis the Eldest. Ellis the Excellent. Ellis of the WASPy yellow-blond hair, who was smart and athletic and had the slim, arched feet of Roman statuary, the perfect SAT score in math. Ellis the boy. Sib had grown up with four brothers and boys were what she knew. Of daughters, she had no idea. She saw Katie and her two sisters as imperfect little hers.

Katie was fourteen and already spending a lot of time at a friend's house when Ellis drowned and Sib went fully AWOL for months, staying in her room with her green tumbler of spiked Hawaiian Punch.

Christine Tyler was Katie's best friend then—and still is. Christine and her parents quietly and warmly absorbed Katie into their family. She ate and slept there maybe half the time throughout high school. Phil and Sib didn't fight it. Oh, Sib made remarks ("What's your fancy Mrs. T. have that I don't?"), but Katie knew better than to respond. Mrs. Tyler let Katie sit in on Christine's tutoring sessions for the SATs; she took her along on Christine's college tour; she helped with Katie's application essays. Katie went to Sarah Lawrence; Christine, to Brown. Christine was now at Yale getting her PhD in physical chem; Katie was in her third year in med school at NYU.

If Mrs. Tyler had so much as a stomachache, Katie would take a leave to care for her. When Katie had called her to say she'd be home for a few days because Sib was dying, Mrs. Tyler, in her typical gentle way, suggested Katie think of what she might say to Sib while she still had the chance. "You two have a complicated relationship," she said, "but maybe come up with a few good memories, some things that you're grateful for." Katie's first thought was, *NOTHING*, but during an interminable three-hour procedure on the second-to-the-last day of her rotation, as she held a patient's bowel away from his gallbladder so the surgeon could operate, she recalled how Sib would call out to her in an urgent, even frantic voice, "Katie! Get out here, right now!" Expecting a scolding, she'd slink to the backyard. "Look!" Sib would cry, waving a hand. "Just *look* at that sunset!" Other times it was, "Look! Look at that light on the mountains!" and "Just look at that plum tree in bloom!"

Maybe she'd remind Sib of those summonses. Maybe they'd laugh about how scared Katie had been, and then it was just a sunset or flowers. Or light.

Holding the retractor, Katie had stood at a forty-five-degree angle to the patient, so she couldn't see what the surgeon was doing—this is the famous endurance test of the gen-surge rotation—and she thought too of all the museums and plays and concerts Sib dragged them to and how she, Katie, now had a taste for such things. Same with the camping trips and piano lessons: the past few summers she'd camped with friends in the Adirondacks, and on her breaks at the hospital, she'd sneak into the ever-empty chapel to play the piano there—and sometimes people drifted in to listen. (When she'd played the Steinway at home last December, Sib said, "Still quite the key basher, Katie-O.")

Perhaps it was not so ironic, then, that there she was, retractor in hand, caring for a stranger while, a continent away, her own mother was mortally ill.

But Sib had Sally and Eva there to drag along through her hideous, self-inflicted ordeal.

Those two, inseparable despite their nine-year age gap, picked her up in Sally's battered orange Datsun station wagon. Katie shoved her overnight bag in the far back between a wooden easel and sacks of fabric. Sally was an art major at Pasadena City College and the car smelled of linseed oil, turpentine, and food.

Eva slipped into the back seat so Katie could sit shotgun. Lanky and pretty at ten, with chin-length thick brown hair, Eva hung her skinny arms over their seat backs. "There's fried chicken for you, Katie-O," she said, and tugged Katie's ponytail.

"We went to Pann's for breakfast," Sally said. "Waffles and chicken. We got you a Coke, too."

With them, there was always some pleasure in the mix.

Eva offered her a paper napkin, then an open bag. She took a drumstick. Greasy, salty, delicious.

She'd left her Cobble Hill apartment in the dark, and it was barely noon here in Los Angeles, a cool, cloudy day.

"Sib's pretty bad," Sally said. "So you know. She weighs, like, eighty-four pounds."

"Yeah, you can see the bones and knobs in her arms and stuff," said Eva.

"And mentally?" Katie asked.

"Oh, Sib's still Sib—even a little rowdy."

"Rowdy?"

"She jokes a lot."

"*Sib?*"

"She was always funny when she wanted to be," said Sally.

"Not in my experience."

"Well, she's funny now," said Sally. "In her own weird way."

Katie didn't see how dying of probably preventable metastatic breast cancer could be funny.

"Anyway, seeing her might be a shock," said Sally.

The sky was full of high, torn-apart clouds; it must have rained in the night because the city looked damp and scoured. "Oh look, look!" Eva said, sounding more than a little like Sib. Beyond downtown's skyscrapers, the gray-violet San Gabriels were capped with snow.

Now that she didn't live with them, Katie enjoyed her sisters. As their own small society of two, they were chatty, sweet, affectionate, and always making things—drawings, sewing projects, food. On the Pasadena Freeway, Eva told them about fifth grade—the band of obnoxious boys who roved the playground insulting the girls, and the mean girls who liked those boys and joined in their cruelty. Katie told them about performing an appendectomy. "Usually, the surgeons make the interns do it, but this guy—he was old and maybe he thought I was the intern—he ordered me through it, step by step. He was really harsh and impatient, but I did it!"

"You cut someone open?" Eva gripped her shoulder.

"I made the incision, yes," Katie said. "But everything is all covered up except for a sterilized area, like, this big." She tapped the console between the two front seats. "So you don't think that much of the actual human."

Sally said that Phil was going to try to be home when they got there, but he might be a little late. Esteban, the hospice nurse, was with their mother right now. "He's just adorable," she said.

"Sally has a crush," said Eva.

"A tiny one," said Sally.

Katie said, "So how's Dad doing?"

"Stoic," said Sally. She pronounced it "stoyk," but Katie didn't correct her.

Katie had never understood how their kind, mild, easygoing father put up with their mother. He was so patient with her short temper, her irritability. Her meanness. Like, here she was dying because mammograms bothered her (and cancer didn't?), and he didn't blame her. "Maybe catching it earlier would have helped," he told Katie last Christmas. "But it's a nasty, treacherous, horrifying disease, so who knows?"

She knew, or thought she did.

Sally pulled into the driveway. "We'll get your things," she said. "Go on in. Sib will want to see you right away."

What if she didn't want to see Sib right away? She pushed

open the heavy front door, then slipped into the hall bathroom—the kids' bathroom. She peed and washed her hands. How wan and mussed she looked. Pulling out her scrunchie, she wound her big fluff ball of a ponytail into a bun. Her old drawer still held some bobby pins and released its familiar scent of the violet soap a great aunt gave her years ago; indeed, two small faded blue ovals still rolled around in the back. (Who gives a twelve-year-old gift soap?) She subdued stray strands of her hair with pins, made an annoyed face at the mirror, and went down the hall to her parents' bedroom.

A hospital bed had replaced their queen. Dining room chairs were lined against the far wall. The drapes were drawn; the only light slipped in from the high clerestories. Sib turned her head—skullish and bright-eyed. "My Katie," she said, and Katie, covering her face, wept.

Did anybody tell you?"

Katie had collected herself and pulled a chair closer to the bed. "Tell me what?"

"Good. I told them I wanted to tell you myself."

"Okay." Katie waited.

"I'm going to take the potion."

"What potion?"

"Dilaudid. To die."

What? "How . . . how can you do that?"

"Oh, I have a stash."

Stash? Since when did Sib talk like a stoner? "Did a doctor give it to you?"

"It was prescribed, yes, if that's what you mean."

What did she mean? Diffuse, inarticulable objections filled her mind like a cloud of gnats. The illegality. The necessity—wasn't she dying anyway? "But why, Mom?"

"Good question. Why, indeed. Let's see. How to put it. Unremitting pain?"

Katie knew the hospice nurse came and gave Sib morphine shots every six hours. "Doesn't hospice keep you comfortable?"

"Oh, sweetie, you're just starting out in life so I don't expect you to understand," said Sib. "You probably still think medicine is the answer to everything, but I'm all tuckered out. I can't make it through a newspaper article, much less a book. I can't follow a TV show. And people have to carry me to the toilet."

"Oh, Mom. They don't mind."

"*I* mind."

"But—" Katie wanted to say, *What about us?* What she said was, "What about Dad?"

"Another good question. What about Phil? Who do you think he'll marry next?"

"Mom!"

"I'm thinking Joan Pomerantz. She's a good cook, has a good sense of humor. And she's rich! They could really trip the light fantastic together. Or there's Melody Rhodes. He's always liked her, she's so tiny and silly. After me, nobody'd blame him for marrying a bimbo."

"Melody's not a bimbo. But Mom, I can't believe—"

"You'll see. The second I'm incinerated there'll be a line out the door of women bearing casseroles."

"Please don't talk like that."

"Like what?"

"*Incinerated.*"

Sib gave a little laugh!

"I don't see what's so funny."

"Oh, honey." Sib wagged her fingers for Katie's hand. Katie gave it to her. Sib's grip was dry and hot and bony; she squeezed Katie's fingers, then let go. And curled in pain.

Katie sat there, helpless, waiting for the spasm to pass. Finally, Sib unclenched and opened her eyes. "Sorry, honey," she whispered, panting.

"Oh, Mom," said Katie. "You know, I always thought that when I had kids, I'd call you every day just to tell you, I don't know, what the baby ate, and you . . ."

Sib squinted at her, as if peering around the pain. "I can't right now," she whispered. "I need to rest."

You were right about the weird jokiness," Katie told Sally in the kitchen.

"It's the morphine talking."

"So is she serious about the Dilaudid?"

"She's been planning it for months."

When her sisters were in the room with Sib, one or the other climbed right on the bed beside her, shoulder to shoulder. They held her hand, they brushed her hair and rubbed lotion on her arms and legs, her swollen ankles, her dried-out feet. Sib hummed with gratitude. Katie admired such devotion but she, the doctor-in-training, could barely kiss Sib's cheek or touch her hand. She'd seen far more grisly cases in the hospital, of course—suppurating sores, hideous open wounds, splintered bone—and felt only interest and concern. But Sib's thick, yellow toenails, her purple swollen ankles, the speckled sun-damaged skin hanging off her bones repulsed her. She tried to get past this—*Come on, Katie, rub a little lotion or you'll hate yourself later*—but she couldn't make herself pick up the Nivea.

So when will she do it?" Katie was with her father in the car. Sally was making hamburgers and had sent them out to buy ketchup, pickles, and buns.

"Soon." Phil was still in his white button-down from work, though he'd taken off his jacket. He looked tired and older, faded. "She wants us all there. We knew you'd have a little time between rotations—"

"But I don't have any time, not a minute! I'll have to make up all these days with double shifts. And you said she was dying, not killing herself . . . and I'm not sure I want any part in that. And I can't believe you've timed it to my schedule, or what you imagine my schedule to be."

"I'm sorry, honey." His eyes, as ever, were so kind and

loving—Sib, with indelible scorn, called them "big ole puppy dog eyes."

"I just can't . . . can't take it in," she said. "How you guys are going along with her when it's completely illegal. And her being so flip."

"That's how she copes," he said. "And it will probably be Saturday, because I'll be home, you're here, and the girls don't have school."

This was Thursday! "And then how you're scheduling it around stuff . . . that's just weird!" she said.

"People have busy lives."

Outside, the old familiar neighborhood streamed past. The Laughtons' house . . . Charlene Kim's . . . the Wilsons, whose chihuahua, Tinkerbelle, had terrorized them every time they walked to school and back; the memories clustered into a deep, sad ache. "So how did Sib get this so-called potion?"

"Her doctor prescribed it. He wasn't very subtle. I was there. He said, 'Now Sibyl, I'm giving you a good amount. Be careful not to take too much at once. Anything over three, four hundred milligrams is very dangerous on top of your usual injections.'"

"And you're okay with this, Dad?"

"She's been in truly unbearable pain."

"Hospice and the morphine should be handling that," she said. Esteban was there right now, injecting her again. Fluffing her pillows.

Phil touched her arm. "If it's too much, honey, you don't have to—"

"It's not too much! It's wrong. But I'm here. I'll see it through."

In all four rotations so far, Katie had yet to see anyone die. A woman in her surgery cohort was present when a man died and she swore there was a shimmering flash. Someone else in her cohort, a guy, said that the death he saw was not so *transcendent*: "The man's system slowed down more and more until it just stopped."

Katie said, "Isn't Eva too young to watch her mother die?"

"Gwen has been talking to her all along and she's on call to take her on Saturday if Eva starts feeling overwhelmed."

Gwen Romero was their next-door neighbor and a shrink.

What Katie wanted to say then was, *So who else knew about this long before I did?* What she said was, "Wow. You guys sure have everything figured out."

At the market, Katie went to find the hamburger fixings while Phil went to the liquor counter. Sib wanted to go out with a drink, her drink: Hawaiian Punch and vodka in the green plastic tumbler that for years had never left her hand from the moment she got home from work till she fell asleep at night—she somehow replenished it without anyone seeing. She was rarely noticeably drunk. But they'd been oblivious.

When Katie was in college, Sib went to AA a few times, then

said she didn't fit in. "I'm just a little ole sipper, and those guys are guzzlers!" Everyone in the meetings, Sib said, had to find a higher power. An HP. "But I already had mine: Hawaiian Punch!"

Maybe she'd always made jokes. They just weren't funny.

Katie thought that the dining room chairs along the wall in Sib's room had been set out for visitors. But that's where the family now ate.

Sib struggled to open her mouth wide enough to bite into her burger, then removed the top bun. She was uncharacteristically quiet. She had always monologued at the dinner table. When Katie was little, Sib had gossiped with gusto about the neighbors—relating confidences she'd extracted about their problem children and miserable marriages. "When Ed Roberts admitted he was having an affair, Lois slammed her tumbler of bourbon smack against his jaw!" When Gwen Romero was studying to become a psychologist, she gave everyone in the neighborhood IQ tests; Sib had coaxed the results out of her and regaled them with the scores of their playmates: the Boyer girls were subaverage, in the low 90s, while Ramona Romero had a surprising 115. "Don't worry," Sib added. "You kids are stratospheric compared to all of them." Phil had listened closely and if Sib paused, or took a sip or a bite, he might offer an opinion: "Lois has often seemed on the verge of violence." Or "I wouldn't broadcast those scores around the neighborhood,

Sib." Then Sib'd be off and running again, waving her fork, excoriating friends and acquaintances. Once she started teaching, her focus moved to the faculty room, to the lives and idiocies of her colleagues. Was the third-grade teacher, Burt Kunholtz, gay or just a mama's boy? Doris Jones, a "health food nut," was eating raw garlic to ward off colds—"You can smell her coming from a mile out!" Even her best work friend, Angela Carlyle, was fair game: "I wish to God Ange'd do something with her hair." They were her captive audience, and her tone, so confidential and self-righteous, made Katie want to explode. (Only years later did she realize Sib was drunk. Even when Sib fell asleep at the dinner table—passed out, slumped in her chair—nobody connected it to the green tumbler.)

These days Sib sipped ice water from a yellow, hospital-issue, covered plastic cup with a built-in straw.

Setting her barely tasted burger on the nightstand, she said, "So. About my ashes . . ."

She'd already made arrangements with the Neptune Society to be cremated and had received, as part of the package, a dark brown leatherette box for her "cremains." "I know if I'm not clear about what I want, there'll be three boxes in the living room."

Ellis's ashes had been in a box in the cabinet under the bookshelves for the past twelve years. With him now was a much smaller box with Hinky's ashes; she'd died last year at sixteen.

"I'd like to be *sprinkled* on the forest floor," Sib said. "Into pine needles or redwood duff. Maybe under some giant sequoias."

"Oh, Mom!" cried Sally.

"Of course, if you keep me in the cabinet with Ellis and Hinky, I'll never know."

"Don't worry, sweetheart," said Phil. "We'll honor your wishes."

Evicted from the marital bedroom when the hospital bed arrived, Phil had been sleeping in Katie's old room, but he insisted on moving to the sofa during her visit. Frankly, she was relieved to be in her old bed. In her old room. With the door shut.

She'd spent her childhood in this room. To some extent, even today, wherever she was, she was still in that room.

Esteban arrived at eight a.m. A compact, kind, soft-spoken man in his thirties, he worked deftly, shooing them out before taking Sib to the toilet, giving her a sponge bath, and injecting her with morphine.

Because Katie was home, Socorro, who usually watched Sib, had the day off. Sally was at Pasadena City College, Eva at Grant Elementary, Phil at Parsons Engineering. Katie sat with Sib as she dozed, and attempted to read *Mansfield Park*, but the room was too dim. When Sib woke, Katie tried to come up with good memories, things she was grateful for. It was true that now, thanks to Sib, she loved museums, the smaller and more peculiar the better. Sib used to dig obscure guidebooks out of the library so that, on road trips, she could take the family to some little farm machinery museum or a museum of whips and brushes. Katie remembered a chicken zoo, a warren of filthy pens and sorry-looking birds. And in a tiny, private taxidermy museum in St. George, Utah, the taxidermist had staged not only wildlife scenes with his work but also a domestic scene with his former pets: an Airedale sat at a desk smoking a pipe while an aproned spaniel carried in a tea tray and cats curled on chair seats. And once—Sib had a special educator's pass—the two of them went on a private, backroom tour of the Natural History Museum, where they saw people reconstructing animal skeletons with tweezers, vitrines of pinned beetles and butterflies, and shelf upon shelf of formaldehyde-yellow bottled specimens: snakes, rat-sized centipedes, and assorted defective fetuses—twin calves, two-headed pigs, and fused human triplets. Katie had loved it—they both had. Then, in the car on the way home, Sib said, "God, Katie, roll down your window. You stink. Why don't you use deodorant?"

Katie was eleven then; she had only the faintest idea of what deodorant was, let alone how to get it or use it.

Sib couldn't help herself; she undercut any good, tender moment.

Katie had learned to steel herself. To hold herself apart.

Sib stirred. "Katie, hon, you know what I'm hankering for? Pancakes."

Katie was not a cook. She had never made a pancake in her life. But she found some Bisquick and a metal mixing bowl and beat in the eggs, oil, and milk. The first three pancakes were blackened blobs, but she cleaned the pan and began again, and the last few were credible, roundish and golden brown.

"Delicious," said Sib. She ate maybe a third of one.

Katie went to open the drapes to let some light into the dusky room.

"Don't," Sib cried, flapping her hand. "Keep them shut."

Esteban came again at two, took Sib to the toilet, straightened her bedclothes, and gave her another injection. "Is there any way we could take her outside?" Katie said. "It's so stuffy and stale in here. She used to love lying out in the sun."

"I've tried," said Esteban. "She said seeing the world makes her sad."

"We could at least open the sliders behind the drapes, get in some fresh air."

"She doesn't like to hear the birds and cars," he said. "That makes her sad too."

Katie and Sib both dozed on and off through a Peter Lorre Mr. Moto movie so old and grainy even the sound was fuzzy. Around three thirty, Sib's former principal, Mrs. Wright, and her teacher friend, Angela Carlyle, came to see her. Katie brought them a pot of tea and left the three to talk shop. Esteban had set a fifteen-minute limit on visits, but she didn't feel comfortable enforcing this. Tall, queenly Mrs. Wright had always intimidated her. The visitors stayed for an hour. When

Katie went back in after they left, Sib was sitting up, alert. Katie gathered the teacups and picked up the tray. "So tell me, sweetheart," said Sib. "Is there anyone special in your life?"

Katie pretended not to hear and carried away the tray. She never told her mother anything personal and had never once brought a boyfriend home. Sib had been rough enough with the few school friends she'd had over—"Kevin, why don't you cut your hair, or brush it, or—heaven forbid—try washing it?" . . . "Why Mimi, you're just bursting out of that top!" Once, when Anne Preston was spending the night, Sib had spooned baking soda into Anne's sneakers. "They stank to high heaven."

Katie never dared put a boyfriend in her path.

"No?" said Sib, when Katie went back into the room. "Should I take that to mean nobody's captured your heart?"

If she kept ignoring her, Katie thought, she might regret it later. "Med school doesn't leave much time for relationships, Mom. But I do like the surgery intern, Gavin. He's incredibly smart and everyone says he's already a talented surgeon."

"A surgeon! What every mother longs to hear! See if he has a friend for Sally—she'll need a high earner to keep her in art supplies!"

This reminded Katie of something else she'd decided to say to Sib: "You know Mom, I'm so glad you always told us to find work that we loved, that we shouldn't settle—"

"Oh god, Katie. Save the elegies. Please." Sib closed her eyes. "I have to rest. Those women wore me out."

Sally and Eva came home and started dinner, chicken stew. Sally, in an apron with her skimpy braids and long skirt, looked like a milkmaid in a nineteenth-century painting. Katie tried to help, but she was so inept chopping an onion, Sally took over and finished in a sec. "I can't believe they let you near a scalpel," she said.

"Scalpels are a lot easier to use," said Katie. "For one, they're sharp."

Eva went to check on Sib and came back. "Sib wants to see the three of us."

Duly, they turned off the burners and filed in.

"Katie, get my jewelry drawer," said Sib. "Just pull the whole thing out. I want to make sure you each get a little something."

"Oh, Mom," said Sally, and her eyes brimmed with tears.

Which made Katie's eyes brim, and Eva's, too.

Most of the drawer held big, clacking necklaces the girls had bought for her as gifts over the years. Sib went for the large shapes and bright colors, claiming that her students appreciated visual variety—which was also her excuse for compulsively buying new clothes. In the far back of the drawer, though, was a quilted box from which she pulled out a gold curb-link bracelet. "Too heavy and garish for me, but my mother wore it every day. Katie, it's yours if you want it. You could always have it melted down and made into, I don't know, a gold medal for all your achievements."

"Yeah, right," Katie said, taking the bracelet, which, as a child, she had seen on Grandma Shula's wrist, the yellow gold gleaming dully against her pale, blue-veined, tissue-paper skin.

"Here are the pearls your father bought for me in Saudi—God knows what possessed him. They're the real thing, not cultured. When I had them restrung, the jeweler said that they're very good, like, eight or nine on a scale of ten, ten being the absolute best. Dad brought you pearls then too, Katie, so Sally gets these."

Katie's Saudi pearls were two strands of pink seed pearls, nothing like the glowing orbs dripping off her mother's hand. Sally took them and carefully slipped them on; long, if not quite opera length, they suited her Pre-Raphaelite look.

"You girls can horse-trade later," said Sib. "As for you, Eva-diva—here's Ellis's class ring. It's a clunker, but that's a real sapphire. You can wear it on this chain, with my rings." Sib's fingers had grown too skinny for the modest fourteen-carat-gold bridal set—what their dad could afford thirty-odd years ago—so he'd bought her a gold chain (itself worth far more than the rings) so Sib could wear them around her neck. Sally helped her get the chain off over her head and gave it to Eva.

"Eva, take my cello, too, if you're serious about wanting to play it. Katie, you can have the piano whenever you have a place for it—I'll tell Dad not to fight you for it. Sally, I don't know what that leaves you. . . ."

"I'm fine," she said.

"Oh, I know, take my mother's silver. A fortune of Georg

Jensen Pyramid. Dad won't ever use it. Take it and put it somewhere before Joan Pomerantz gets her hands on it. Or pawn it and get yourself a decent car. Everything else, clothes, shoes—you girls take what you want and give the rest to Socorro and Goodwill. There's also a fortune in perfume your father bought in duty-free and every last bit of it makes me sneeze. Take it, use it, sell it, give it away. Okay. Now, what's for dinner?"

Around eight on Saturday morning, Esteban came into the kitchen, where the sisters were sitting at the counter drinking coffee. "She's down to eighty-two pounds," he said.

Katie quietly asked how long he thought Sib had.

"She's tough, it could be anytime—or days, even weeks," he said. "And how're all of you doing? Anything you need, anything I can do for you?"

No, no, they said, and thanked him—again—for his kindness.

"Your all being here is wonderful support for her, and for each other, I'm sure," he said. "Yours is the kind of loving family that I don't see often enough."

They nodded like bobblehead dash ornaments.

Apparently, Katie thought, going through the motions looked like love.

Esteban said he'd be back at two.

So this was it. It. Phil went in to talk to Sib; after fifteen minutes, Sally peeked in and reported back, "They're holding each other, just crying and crying." After ten more minutes, Phil emerged red-eyed and shaky and began making a pitcher of Hawaiian Punch. "She wants everyone to have a glass with her."

"Okay, but make mine a virgin," Sally said. Eva and Katie echoed that.

They filed into the room. Each held a sturdy, clear drinking glass, except for Sib, who'd kept one of her talismanic green plastic tumblers, into which their father now poured magenta-red Hawaiian Punch.

"Stop!" Sib cried when it was half-full.

A fifth of vodka and a brown prescription bottle sat out on her night table. She struggled with the brown bottle's child-proof lid. Sally moved to help, but Sib waved her off. "I don't want anyone ever thinking they had a hand in this." She finally got the top off and poured dollops of syrup into her punch. She held the bottle up to see how much was left, then added a few more dollops. "That'll do it," she said, and poured in a few good glugs of vodka. "For the taste I love," she said. "Anyone else?" She offered the clear flat bottle around the room. "No-body? Okay then." She raised the green tumbler in a toast. "Thank you all for being here," she said, and took her first sip.

"Sure you're ready, Mom?" said Katie.

"Beyond ready, sweetie." Sib took a few quick swallows. "Not bad." She drank some more. "Ahhh, HP, my favorite," she said, then, "Remember—pine needles or redwood duff." She drank in long gulping swallows, stopped to pant, until she finished it off. She set down the empty tumbler and nodded. "Okay then," she said, tucked her chin to her chest, and closed her eyes.

Sally and Eva each took a hand. Their dad went behind the bed and slid his arms around Sib's neck, kissing the top of her head. Fighting her aversion, Katie put her hand on Sib's shin, on top of the blanket. Sib opened her eyes, squinted at everyone, and shut them again. She did this several times, her gaze less and less focused. Once, she stirred, as if trying to sit up, and gazed blearily around the room. "Where's Hinky?" she said. "Hinky? Hinky? Oh, there you are! Come on, come here." Freeing her hand that Eva held, Sib patted the blanket. "That's a good girl." Her eyelids fluttered shut. Her facial muscles flexed; sometimes she nodded or slightly shook her head.

There was work to dying, Katie could tell, to withdrawing from life, to finding the way out; she had a sense of long corridors, a narrow path over rocky ground, a dark forest closing in. How far away a person can go even when they're there, right in front of you! They all held on to Sib, but could accompany her only so far; at some point—at the banks of the dark river—she had to go on alone.

Sally whispered, "She's stopped squeezing back."

They held on to her, still, as her breathing slowed.

And slowed even more. In the long pauses between inhales, her face was still.

"She's in her deep sleep," their father said, and moved away.

They pulled up the chairs and sat close around her. She never struggled. She breathed maybe three times a minute.

Sometimes tears rolled down their cheeks, and sometimes they gave each other wondering looks—was the potion working?

Sally took their drinking glasses and brought them back clean, along with a pitcher of ice water to dilute the lingering, cloying sweetness of Hawaiian Punch—to this day Katie can't bear fruit punch of any kind. Their father cleared away the Dilaudid, the vodka, the green tumbler, which was smart because Esteban showed up earlier than expected, at noon. "I just had a feeling she was close," he said, and after taking her pulse and timing her breath, he said, "She's even closer than I thought. It won't be long."

They studiously avoided looking at one another.

She was soon down to breathing twice a minute. Each breath was a surprise. Katie knew, and Esteban knew, that when someone breathes like that, there's no going back. They never left her all alone, but she was taking so long to die, they began going in and out of the room. Esteban stayed for two and a half hours, then had to go to his next patient. "I'll come back as soon as I can."

Katie was folding laundry with Eva in the living room and their father was on the phone to one of Sib's brothers when Sally called out: "Dad! Eva! Katie!"

Esteban had left a stethoscope. Phil listened for a heartbeat. "Gone," he said. It was three fifteen in the afternoon.

The Neptune Society sent two young men to pick up Sib's body. Their ill-fitting, shabby black suits, marijuana reek, and affected formality got Katie and Sally giggling, and when the two guys had trouble maneuvering the body through the heavy, self-closing front door, the sisters had to duck into the kitchen to stop laughing.

Phil made phone calls, inviting people to the memorial service on Monday at the community center, and to sit shiva after that. Gwen and Troy Romero and their daughter, Ramona, came over with a lasagna and salad that everyone ate with savage appetites. They told Sib stories—the high-pitched way she'd called Hinky that the neighborhood kids mercilessly imitated; the lemon meringue pie she made for Troy's birthday one year where she'd accidently used salt for sugar; her favorite expressions: *gadzooks! . . . oh, for crying in the bucket . . . don't do anything drastic.* They laughed, and swept away tears, then planned the memorial.

Funny how the days you weep, you can also have the fullest, deepest laughs.

The memorial service was short and well attended, and afterward people came over to the house, where great quantities of food and wine arrived thanks to neighbors and friends. Queenly Mrs. Wright brought a bottle of good Scotch, which she drank with the men.

Katie's best friend, Christine, was back east, but her parents, Mrs. and Mr. Tyler, brought a cheese platter and stayed for hours.

"I took your advice and tried to tell Mom some stuff," Katie told Mrs. Tyler. "But she didn't want to hear it."

"You tried and that's what's important. But to go through with what she did, it must have taken everything she had. All her focus and determination."

Sally, carrying a plate of blintzes, caught Katie's eye and tipped her head: Joan Pomerantz had just walked in bearing a large blue enameled pot.

Almost three years later, Phil's girlfriend invited them over for Christmas Day at her La Crescenta condominium.

Phil had sidestepped both Joan Pomerantz and Melody Rhodes and wound up with a Pam. A shiksa. An HR person he knew from Parsons. She'd gone after him and he'd acquiesced. Sally and Eva and Katie didn't like her—among themselves, with wanton immaturity, they called her IckyPam. Brisk and managerial, she seemed too chilly for their sweet father, and too interested in money; she'd talked him into taking an investment course, though it wasn't clear that she herself had much to invest. Now Phil was talking about her moving in with him and Eva. But that day, they were all in Pam's too clean, too beige condo, with more knickknacks than books on the shelves. Phil was cheery, pouring drinks. Eva and Sally brought homemade gifts, a gorgeous ceramic platter for Pam and linen place mats and napkins for Katie and Gavin, who was on duty at Cedars and couldn't be there. Pam's twenty-year-old son, Jason, a computer-programming student, sat on the sofa watching football with the sound off.

Pam was making an effort, so the sisters did too: that is, Pam served HoneyBaked ham and the sisters ate some. Katie left early; now she, too, had to go to work. She'd decided on psychiatry and her residency was in the locked ward at UCLA.

She'd walked maybe halfway to her car down the condo's long eucalyptus-lined driveway when it occurred to her that everything was okay. She could stop fighting the way things had turned out. It was still sad that Sib had died and unfortunate that Phil was with IckyPam (so far), but somehow, she no longer had to resist or protest these facts. Everything was all right. She stood still to absorb this idea—and test it. Birds rustled and chirped in the trees, a squirrel chittered at her, cars hummed down on the road. Yes: It was okay that their father liked Pam even if she and her sisters didn't. It was even okay that Sib was dead—especially since there was nothing to be done about it. She had been sad and haunted about Sib, and worried about her father for a long while, and now, somehow, she could let up. Relax the vigil. Because all was well. Well enough. The world still ached with beauty. The birds kept chirping, leaves clattered in a breeze, the late-afternoon sunlight, thick and pale, slanted in from the south. Maybe a shimmer of sadness persisted, but wouldn't it always, and wouldn't she want it to?

"Okay then," Katie said aloud, and walked the rest of the way to her car, got inside, and drove to work.

Remembering and Repeating

Eva Samuelson had been accepted at three of the four colleges she'd applied to: UC Berkeley, Stanford, and Pomona. She hadn't gotten into her first choice, which was Caltech. She'd gone to high school right across the street from Caltech and had two summer internships in a physics lab there. She'd assumed that, come September, she could keep living with her sister Sally, steer a block north for school, and life as she loved it could go on with no luck-of-the-draw roommates, no dining hall mystery meat.

Not even on the wait list.

The prof who'd supervised her in the physics labs said admissions didn't accept that many locals and that she should've applied to MIT.

Even before Caltech rejected her, she'd had a creeping bad feeling about college, a low drumming dread, which was another reason why she'd wanted to make the tiniest transition possible, one so negligible that fate might not notice. Before she was born, her father, Ellis Samuelson, drowned the day before his college classes started. Who was to say something like that wouldn't happen to her?

Weird things repeated in families. In *her* family. For example: when both her birth mom and her birth mom's mother were pregnant, their babies' fathers died tragically before they ever saw their kids. Coincidence or pattern? Who'd want to find out?

In the seventh grade, during sex ed week, it was drummed into them how girls born to teenage mothers were exponentially more likely to become teenage mothers themselves. Again, her birth mother, Julia Ortiz, was born to a seventeen-year-old, and Julia herself accidently got pregnant when she was barely twenty, so pretty much the same thing.

Eva's boyfriend, Wally Granger, was lobbying her for sex, and that, too, fueled her dread.

Sex and college. Both could be her doom. And Wally's.

Eva knew, of course, that all these fears were probably silly and superstitious, so she didn't tell anybody about them, not even her sister Sally, her favorite human being.

Another reason this college business was getting out of hand was because Sally wanted her to go one place, and her birth mother, Julia, wanted her to go someplace else. There would be no pleasing both.

BUG HOLLOW

Sally said she'd take Eva to visit the schools up north during spring break, the second week of April. They'd drive up the coast, make a holiday of it. Eva suggested they stay with Julia in Walnut Creek, but Sally said a hotel would be more fun.

Eva had lived with Sally her entire life, except for the first three months Sally was in her first apartment, a leafy, charming bungalow court in Pasadena. Even then, Eva was over there a lot. When their father's girlfriend Pam moved in with their dad, Eva began staying at Sally's more of the time. Not that her dad and Pam forced her out. More, the situation suited everyone: Pam liked having Phil to herself, and Sally and Eva were happiest living together. What finally clinched the deal was that Eva's new high school was walking distance from Sally's place, so Eva spent weeknights there and some weekends at her dad's.

Sally at twenty-seven had an MFA in ceramics and textile art. Slim and pale, with fine, dark blond hair, she was very intelligent and sensitive, and clever with her hands. She'd developed a technique of quilting paper, usually pages from magazines and newspapers, then washing it, ending up with webs of thread or string with bits of text and images caught like flies in beautiful, haunting ways. She'd spent one summer working for a draper and now, to make a living, she sewed custom blinds and curtains in a small rented shopfront studio, where she made art in the mornings and sewed window coverings for her clients in the afternoons. When she had no orders, she made stuffed toys, napkins, and place mats that she and Eva sold at craft fairs.

Sally's boyfriend, Charlie, was at the bungalow almost every night. He was still at ArtCenter, finishing a graduate degree in transportation design. A serious pot smoker, he lit up with his morning coffee, then every few hours till bed. He'd tried reining it in to please Sally, but that never lasted long. They'd been together for two years.

Often, the three of them—Charlie, Sally, and Eva—sat at the dining room table after dinner, two of them drawing as Eva did homework. Sally put out nuts and chocolate and brewed herbal teas. Charlie played mixtapes with Joni Mitchell, the Cowboy Junkies, Jane's Addiction. Sally once looked up and said, "This is the heaven of our life," and that's how Eva thought of it too.

A week before they left on the college tour, Eva found Sally crying in the kitchen, wiping her face on her apron like a fairy-tale person. At first, Sally said she was crying about Charlie; then she blurted, "And you're leaving in the fall!"

When Eva told some of her friends about this, they said their mothers were also bursting into tears all over the place for the same reason: their girls would soon be gone.

Eva had till May 1 to decide on a college. A month.

Julia, her birth mom, lobbied hard for Berkeley because it was her alma mater and half an hour away from her house in Walnut Creek. "You'll like a home-cooked meal from time to time."

Sally leaned Pomona because it was half an hour from her.

Eva did love the old California feel of Claremont, the eucalyptus trees, the Spanish-style buildings, and Mount Baldy right there, like a big snow-covered god.

They decided to take the 101, the fast coastal route. "And, if you want," Sally said, "we could stop at Bug Hollow on the way."

"Yes!" Bug Hollow was the old hunting lodge in the Santa Cruz Mountains where Eva's birth parents had lived together, and she was conceived. She'd always wanted to see the place.

"And while we're at it," Sally added, "maybe we could scatter Ellis's ashes."

"Okay," Eva said, not giving it much thought. She had a lot going on right then: she and her girlfriends were in frantic discussions about which college to go to; they'd decide one day and change their minds the next. Plus, Eva had her *Portrait of a Lady* paper to write and three midterms before the break. And then, there was Wally diving at her waistband.

Sally had long wanted to take Ellis's ashes to Bug Hollow, because he'd told her that his summer there with Julia was the happiest he'd ever been.

The only person opposed to this idea was dead.

Eva's adopted mother, Sib, had considered Bug Hollow the filthy backwoods hideout of the cult that captured Ellis, cut him off from his family, and would have kept him out of college had she not intervened. Even after Sib died and her own ashes were scattered as she'd stipulated under Sequoia redwoods, and their beloved Hinky's ashes had been raked into the back flower bed where she'd loved hunting lizards, Ellis's ashes stayed in the living room cabinet. Dad and Katie had conceded that if Ellis's ashes had to go somewhere, Bug Hollow was as good a place as any, but nobody had gotten around to organizing an expedition.

Wally said, "I was hoping we could go camping over break."

Camping! Ellis had gone on a camping trip when he was Eva's age—and she was the result!

She'd known Wally since ninth-grade math club, but they'd only gotten together this past January. He had small sparkly eyes and a long oval face topped with a tuft of dense red hair that floated left. His goofy laugh—*ayuk ayuk*—sometimes made her laugh so hard, she peed. She loved his pale lips and skinny, blue-white chest and petal-pink nipples, but what-all below his waist was more than she could take on. For now, at least.

In the week before the trip north, Eva had two dreams in which she kept trying to get to college. In one, the steering wheel of the car turned into a flapping palm frond; in the other, she was swimming to school in water that got darker and thicker till she woke up.

Not sure I remember," said Julia, when Eva called her to get directions to Bug Hollow. "I haven't been there for . . . how old are you? Eighteen years. Why are you going *there*?"

"I've always wanted to see it," Eva said. "And to scatter Ellis's ashes."

"Really? Gosh." Silence. "Just the two of you? Nobody else is coming?"

Eva heard wistfulness. "Unless you want to."

"Let me check my schedule," Julia said, brisk again, "and I'll call you back."

Sally wasn't happy that Eva had invited Julia. "Except I bet she won't come," she said. "Every time I mention Bug Hollow to her, she ignores me or changes the subject."

Eva was a three-week-old embryo when her father drowned. Julia hadn't even known she was pregnant for some months after that. And because she was so young, bereft, alone, and broke, and because she did not want to be a single mother like her own mother was, Julia gave Eva to Ellis's parents, who legally adopted her. Phil and Sib were in their early forties then, young enough, they felt, to pass as her parents, so that's what Eva called them, Mom and Dad; though just as often she called them Sib and Phil.

They never lied to her. For as far back as she could remember, Eva knew she was adopted, that Ellis was her birth father and a girl named Julia was her birth mother.

Naturally, Eva had daydreamed about Julia, imagining a joyful first meeting and—especially when Sib was harsh or angry with her—running off to live with Julia in a perfect little cottage in the woods where Julia was the kind, just, loving *real* mother Eva had been denied. Sally had told Eva in secret how pretty Julia was, what a good artist she was, how she'd turned Ellis into a big mush pot. Julia had also anointed Sally an artist and the two had vowed "to be the artists in the family."

Eva finally met Julia a few months after Sib died. Phil gave Eva Julia's address—it turned out he'd been sending her updates and photos all along. Eva wrote and Julia wrote right back—"I've been waiting eleven years for your letter"—and flew down to see her within the week. Julia was so young, and pretty, and affectionate, especially after Sib, who was, after all, her grandmother and strict and then very sick.

Eva and Julia compared their noses and ears, hands and feet, likes and dislikes and were just the same. Eva was ecstatic.

Sally was not.

Sally, by then, was an art major at Oxy. And Julia was no longer an artist but a businesswoman, the CEO of a design firm that outfitted high-end restaurants, hotels, and resorts. More bean counter than designer.

"And she dresses like an executive secretary," Sally said.

Sally knew you couldn't hold people accountable for youthful vows they didn't remember making, but she still considered Julia a corporate sellout with bourgeois taste.

Eva thought Julia perfect.

When Julia invited her to spend the summer in Walnut Creek, she went. She met her little half brothers, Tig, three, and Chris, five; their nanny, Regina; and Julia's husband, Larry, who was in tech. The two huge sleepy Bernese mountain dogs were Mimi and Olaf. None of them—Larry, the boys, the dogs, the nanny—showed the least interest in her. Julia and Larry worked all day; the nanny had her hands full with the boys. Eva sat by the big pool and read both the books she'd brought the first day. Julia came home that night with maybe a hundred dollars' worth of drawing supplies—paper and pastels, and a fancy easel. She'd clearly mixed her up with Sally. (Even at eleven Eva was already a math-and-science person.)

She lasted a week.

The funny thing was, she went right back to idolizing Julia, and whenever Julia wanted to see her or invited all of them for Thanksgiving or Christmas, Eva was thrilled. Not Sally, who never forgave Julia for "going corporate."

For Eva, explaining her family to people had always been complicated, what with the two sets of parents, the smudged generations—grandparents who were parents, aunts who were sisters—plus who was dead, who was alive.

After she heard a song by Willie Nelson called "I'm My Own Grandpa," Eva wrote a song called "I'm My Own Aunt":

My grandma and my grandpa
Took me as their kid
So my dad and their two daughters
All became my sibs

Since my dad was now my brother
His daughter'd be my niece,
So as my father's sister,
I'm an aunt to me!

Chorus:

It seems impossible,
People say I can't
But I'm my own aunt
I'm my own aunt!

"Yes!" Julia said when she called back. She'd meet them in the parking lot of Johnnie's market in the mountain town of Boulder Creek at eleven a.m. on Tuesday and show them the way to Bug Hollow.

Their dad and Katie came to dinner the night before they left. Sally said, "I thought we could scatter Ellis's ashes at Bug Hollow. If that's okay with you guys."

"Without us?" said Katie. "I don't know."

"You can come," Sally said. "Everyone can."

"I have patients." Katie was a psychiatrist and psychoanalyst in Westwood.

"And I'm in Palm Springs all week," their father said. "If you girls could wait . . ."

"His ashes have been in that cupboard for eighteen years," Sally said. "Nobody else has ever done anything with them. Why not just let us do it?"

"Oh, sweetheart, I'm not going to fight you," said their dad. "I wish we could do it all together, but if you're sure you want to take it on . . ."

"It might be more emotional than you think," said Katie. "You might want to hold off for more support."

"Julia's meeting us there," Eva said.

"Really?" Katie said. "That's good. I guess. But I'm sorry I won't be there."

They set off on a sunny Monday morning in high spirits with a thermos of milky coffee in Sally's taxicab-yellow pickup with the camper shell. Their first stop was their childhood home in Altadena, where their father still lived. His girlfriend, Pam, had just moved out after four years. She said that she could never make the place her own and Sib's presence was still too strong in the Danish modern furniture, the grand piano that nobody played, the sturdy Dansk dishes in the cupboards. Also, Pam said, correctly, that his daughters were cold to her.

Except for half a roll of flowered paper towels, the house looked as if Pam had never been there.

Sally turned slowly around in the kitchen. "It's a family curse. Pam left Dad, Gavin left Katie, Charlie's probably leaving me, and soon you'll be gone too."

"Now Sal," said Eva, but her sister's sorrowful tone set her own dread clanging like a church bell.

When Eva was very little, maybe four or five, she tried to plug a Christmas tree bulb into a regular wall socket and got such a terrible shock, she knew she'd electrocuted herself and would soon be dead. She was harrowed with guilt: her death, she knew, would make her parents very sad; she'd destroyed something precious of theirs. (Oddly, she grieved little to none on her own behalf.) She remembered driving somewhere in the car, looking at the backs of Sib's and Phil's heads, and thinking, *Those poor, poor people, they lost one child and now, I've done it to them again.*

When she broke down and told them that she'd electrocuted herself and would soon be dead, they laughed and laughed: "Sweetheart, it doesn't work like that."

Now, about to graduate, she had the same feeling that something inexorable and fatal was on its way and everyone she loved would be hurt.

For the past eighteen years Ellis's ashes had shared a shelf with a blue felt Hanukkah decoration, a measuring tape you couldn't pull out, and a rock that looked like a potato that they sometimes put on people's plates as a joke. Also, a box of Samuelson family photos from the early 1900s: women in stiff black dresses and men with prodigious beards and side curls. Nobody alive knew who any of them were.

Ellis's ashes were wrapped in the shiny off-white paper they came in, with a faded purple ribbon tied around the long way. Eva had sometimes looked in at the box, but it never made her feel anything. Sally lifted it out and handed it to her. She was surprised by how heavy it was. She'd assumed ashes were light—but she must have been thinking of soft, fragile fireplace ashes.

"You think this is okay without Dad and Katie?"

"They said it was okay, especially since Julia's coming. It's not like they ever made a plan to do anything with them. And it's about time someone did."

With the box between them on the bench seat, their mood turned somber and ceremonial, as if they'd become a one-vehicle cortege. Sally had tucked a small, creased copy of Ellis's prom photo under the ribbon: with his loopy blond curls, braces, tux, and buttonhole carnation, he looked young and dweeby. Hard to believe, Eva thought, that three months after that picture was taken, he'd made Julia pregnant—with her! And three weeks after that, the day before his first college class at Ole Miss, he drowned in a tangle of tree branches in a quarry pond.

She was almost as old as he'd ever been.

Sally said, "You're awfully quiet."

"Thinking." Without intending to, she'd moved as far from the box as she could.

They were almost to the freeway when a car cut in front of them. Sally slammed on the brakes and the box slid to the floor by her feet. One-handed, still driving, she dragged it back onto the seat. "Sorry 'bout that, El," she said, patting the top. "Shook you up a bit, eh?"

So they didn't have to be all mopey and funereal! Eva dug around for the middle seat belt and tugged it out. "C'mon, Pops," she said, wrapping one end around the box. "Let's strap you in."

The morning traffic on the 101 North was thinning out, though there were some thick patches through the Valley. The freeway plantings were lush with new growth. "And the Wally update?" said Sally.

Her way of asking if Eva had slept with him yet. "No news."

Sally had taken Eva to Planned Parenthood when she turned sixteen. "Just so you're prepared," she said. But Eva knew that accidents happened even to the prepared: she herself was a case in point.

"You have more self-control than I ever did," Sally said.

"It's just something could go wrong."

"Like what?"

"You know. Pregnancy. Disease."

"Hard to see Wally as a venereal petri dish," said Sally.

This made Eva giggle. "More a venereal virgin," she said.

"Is he?"

"A virgin? Oh, I'm sure."

"You know, you won't get pregnant. You have protection."

"You hear of babies born clutching IUDs."

"Oh, please. That old urban myth?"

Eva couldn't bring herself to mention the other thing: how when Julia and Julia's mother were pregnant, the fathers of those babies—her father and grandfather—both died terrible deaths. "Besides, Wally only got into Ivies," she said. "In four months we'll be on opposite sides of the country. I don't want to start college in a long-distance relationship."

"You are so levelheaded. I always jump in with both feet and hope for the best."

"Is that what you did with Charlie?"

"God, Charlie. I should break up with him before he breaks up with me."

Charlie, Eva knew, had spent the night at their cottage, because his skunky pot smell seeped even under her closed door. "His smoking still bugging you?" she asked.

"I can live with that. But now he says my calves aren't big enough."

"Big enough for what?" said Eva.

"That's what I wanted to know. He couldn't say. Except that he finds big calves hot, like some men go for big breasts. Katie said it might be a mother thing, from babyhood, like when his mom's calves loomed large as he crawled at her feet."

Katie liked giving theoretical assessments of their love lives. Eva had stopped telling her anything personal. "Charlie's a doofus head," she said. How could the girth of Sally's perfectly normal calves trump her love for him, her sweetness, her *cooking*?

Sally was a wonderful cook.

"What do you think, El?" Eva put one ear close to the box, as if listening, then sat up. "Ellis says, if Charlie doesn't love you because of your calves, maybe you better find someone who loves you, calves and all."

"Good advice," said Sally. "But it makes me so fucking sad."

Maybe a mile later, Sally said, "And speaking of sad . . . Last night, Dad asked if we wanted to move home. I thought he might be tired of paying your half of the rent, so I told him I could handle the whole nut. He said it's not about money. He's lonely."

"Oh god." How unbearable to think of their kind, sweet dad being lonely.

"We need to find him a girlfriend," Sally said. "A good one, this time."

They spent the night in a Santa Cruz motel and the next morning drove through bright green pastures and hills of yellow mustard before turning east into the Santa Cruz Mountains. Soon, they were in the pines. When the first redwoods appeared, Sally said, "Look, look at those trees!" sounding on purpose like Sib, who had always instructed them on scenery.

Eva unfastened Ellis's seat belt and held the box above the dashboard. "Look familiar, El?"

The tiny rustic town of Felton went by in seconds; then tree-lined Ben Lomond, Brookdale, and finally they were in dusty, straggly Boulder Creek with its Old West wooden facades. Sally drove slowly, frowning. "I guess it's gone, the Kandy Kone," she said. "Where Ellis worked. But here's Johnnie's."

And there was Julia, standing against her Volvo station wagon, waving at them. She had on a crisp blue-and-white-striped shirt and white jeans. Her hair was in a short, mannish cut: wavy on top, tapered up the back. "Evie," she called out. "Pips!"

Ellis's old nickname for Sally. Only Julia ever called her that.

"Be nice. Please," Eva said, because sometimes neither older woman was.

Sally climbed into the Volvo's back seat, so Eva got in next to Julia and settled the box on her knees.

"That's him?" Julia drew back. "Huh. Not even an urn?"

Sally, in the back seat, mouthed, Save me.

"Hey, El," Eva said, holding him up. "Here's Julia. We're going to Bug Hollow!"

Julia gave her a serious mom frown—*Enough!*

Eva put down the box and shut up.

When it was time for Eva to go to high school, Julia wanted her to move up north and attend a good public school in Walnut Creek. But Eva was accepted at Polytechnic in Pasadena and wanted to go there, in large part so she could live with Sally in her pretty little courtyard unit. Julia worried that Sally, then twenty-four, was too young to be Eva's primary adult, and that Sally's romantic, offbeat, art-focused lifestyle would dull the girl's ambition or somehow misdirect her. Eva heard only Sally's side of their phone call: "It's not my decision. . . . Eva wants to go to Poly. . . . It's the best school in Pasadena. . . . She'll see plenty of her dad. . . . He's fine with it."

Eva had no regrets. She'd liked Poly.

Last October, Julia took her to Todos Santos in Baja for a three-day weekend. They stayed in a small, elegant hotel Julia's firm had furnished; they swam in the infinity pool, took a yoga class, and walked on a beach with such ferocious surf, you couldn't even wade in it. Julia knew by then that Poly was all about academic achievement and funneling students into elite schools, but she wanted to make sure Eva had the necessary oversight and guidance for her college applications. Clearly, Julia hadn't trusted Sally or Phil to be on top of this. But Eva had taken the SATs her junior year, and nobody suggested she needed to raise her scores. She'd drafted her application essay over the summer, fine-tuned it with Sally and Katie and her college counselor in the fall. By the time she and Julia had landed in Cabo, Eva had already sent off applications to the four colleges she liked.

The road to Bug Hollow was paved in soft black asphalt. "This is new," Julia said and drove slowly, peering at houses set back in the trees. Then, "Oh gosh, we're here!" The road had ended in a wide turnaround in front of a large, fog-gray shingled house.

In silence they took in a wide fan of concrete steps—the kind where photos of whole wedding parties could be taken. Up on the porch were white wicker chairs with hot pink cushions and a front door painted a darker, lipstick pink.

Sunk in a flowerbed:

THE DAYDREAM

BED-AND-BREAKFAST

AND

DAY SPA

Sally said, "It used to have dark brown shingles. And the time we drove up, around ten dogs ran down to greet us."

“Five,” Julia said. “Only five dogs.”

“So what do we do now?” Eva said.

“We go in,” said Julia.

They left Ellis in the car.

The door opened into a lobby with a long sleek counter against one wall. A brass luggage rack waited by an elevator. To the left of the entrance, a lounge had cloudy gray walls and sofas with accent pillows in varying pinks. To the right, a dining room had wraparound windows looking out on the treetops. Flutes and a harp played at a low volume. “I know the firm that did this,” said Julia. “Their signature look is tarted up Zendo.”

“Hi there.” A young blond receptionist stood up behind the counter. “Your name? Are you here for the night or the spa?”

“I used to live here, years ago,” Julia said. “And I was hoping to show my daughter and sister-in-law my old home.”

Sister-in-law! Eva elbowed Sally.

“One minute, please.” The receptionist opened a door behind her, said something, and a tall, older woman emerged. “May I help you?”

Julia repeated her wish. “. . . to see the house. The swimming hole out back.”

“You’re free to look around downstairs, but the second floor is the spa and above that are the guest rooms—all off-limits, I’m afraid. As for the swimming hole—floods in the eighties shifted things around back there. You're free to go look, of course."

They wandered into the gray lounge with its low ceilings. Sally said, "I remember dark log beams and big leather sofas. And a lot of shedding taxidermy."

Julia said, "They completely gutted the place. Even the stairs and fireplace are gone. There's nothing left to situate me. I can't tell where the old rooms were."

They went through the dining room, then out into the garden and through a gate to where the swimming hole used to be. Now, there was a dry, rocky wash.

The stream was some fifty yards farther on, through a thicket of cottonwood saplings. The mud brown water ran treacherously high and fast and loud.

Eva yelled over its roar. "We can't leave him here."

Back in the reception area, the older woman came out from behind the counter. "If you like, I can offer you our lunchtime spa package for half price. That's a sauna, and a facial or pedicure." She lowered her voice. "My staff could use the work."

Her staff was the receptionist and another woman who was folding napkins in the dining room.

Julia turned to Sally and Eva. "My treat?"

Minutes later, they were in the sauna. Eva, the last to enter, found Julia stretched out on her towel on the second bench and Sally sitting on the lower, cooler one. Both were naked. Eva sat down at the end of the lower bench and held her towel tightly closed.

Julia nudged her with her toe. "Don't be shy. It's just us."

Eva was used to seeing Sally's nymphlike, long lithe body, her small pretty breasts. Julia was larger than Sally and her—taller and thicker, her breasts full and wide, with dark nipples and a slight droop: a lush, lived-in body. Silvery stretch marks squiggled her belly and hips.

Quickly, Eva was hot in the towel. Very hot. Slowly, she let it drop to her waist.

Another nudge from Julia. "God, look at beautiful perfect you. Ah youth."

Eva quickly pulled her towel up again, covering her breasts.

Julia laughed. "She really has her father's physique, doesn't she?" Julia again touched Eva's shoulder with her toe. "His long lean athlete's body."

"Eva has a butt, though," said Sally. "And hips. With Ellis, there was nothing to hold his pants up. He wore them so low it always seemed that one good tug could bring them down."

"That's about all it took," Julia said and laughed again.

They were soon glistening with sweat. Curls of hair fastened to Julia's forehead. Sally's face was flushed. Eva liked the smell of hot wood but felt woozy. She let her towel slip down again, as she was now too hot to care. They'd set the timer for fifteen minutes, which already was as long as a week. She was sweating into her eyes and growing short of breath.

"It is surreal being back here," Julia said. "It's like one of those dreams where you're someplace familiar, but you keep finding rooms you never knew existed."

Yes, Eva thought. It could be another one of the dreams she'd been having, where she set out for college only to wind up naked and boiling in a wooden box.

"I guess we waited too long to come," said Sally. "Too bad. I always wanted Eva to see where you and Ellis lived that summer."

"You really have a ridiculouly romantic take on that time," Julia said. "Bug Hollow was just a cheap summer student rental: dirty and shabby and perfectly named—crawling with ticks and spiders. Not to mention gnats and mosquitoes!"

"Yes, but the last days I spent with Ellis, you and Bug Hollow were all he talked about. I'm glad he had that happiness before he died. He really loved it here."

"I have to say, I like the place a lot better now."

"Not me," said Sally. "But I'm hardly a spa-going corporate type."

"You guys," Eva said, but she wasn't sure that they heard her.

"You have the luxury to see the past all in a golden haze—Bug Hollow, Ellis and me, you and me doodling. The truth is, Ellis and I were only together for two months. Then, he died. I carried his baby for nine months with him gone for all of it. I had to drop out of school, move home with my mom, and go through labor. All for a baby I couldn't keep and then wasn't allowed to see. That pretty much killed any nostalgia I had about this place. I would have been happy never seeing it again. Although it's much better now."

"So why did you even come today?"

"To support Eva when she scattered her father's ashes."

"I'm fine," Eva said, but they weren't listening to her.

"You always think Eva lacks proper care and supervision—and you're the only person who can give it to her. Never mind how well loved and cared for she's been from birth—long before you showed up."

"I would have been there sooner, except your folks pulled a bait and switch. They promised I could have a relationship with her till I signed the forms; then they wouldn't let me see her."

"Eva doesn't need to hear this," Sally said.

"It's about time she knows. Phil talked me into a standard adoption saying it was easier than a grandparents' custodial arrangement. He said we'd make a visitation plan later. Well, that never happened."

A fan clicked on and a new wave of heat rolled through.

"But you didn't even try to see Eva till she was five!" Sally said. "I know because Mom and Dad had a huge fight about it then. He was all for including you in the family, but Sib felt it would be too confusing for Eva to suddenly have two moms."

"Sib hated me."

"She was only thinking of Eva. Like all of us, she thought that you having Ellis's baby was incredibly generous and loving, especially since if we hadn't agreed to take Eva, you were going to have an abortion. You already had the appointment!"

"Stop it," Eva said. "Both of you."

"I wouldn't have gone through with it," Julia said.

"Who knows what you would have done. But our family took Eva, loved her to pieces, and you got to get your degrees, start your business, marry your tech millionaire. And then, you wanted Eva, too."

"I just want what's best for her."

"And we don't?"

"Jesus, you two!" Eva stood, rewrapped her towel, and left the sauna.

She stood under the cool shower. She'd never heard Sally so angry and reckless. But what Sally said hadn't shocked her. Of course Julia would have considered an abortion, given her situation.

What really annoyed her was being talked about as if she weren't there.

Showers went on in nearby stalls and Eva waited until they were turned off before she got out. In the locker room, Sally and Julia were sitting next to each other on a bench in matching gray terry-cloth robes. They looked equally wide-eyed and abashed.

"Sorry, babe," Julia said. "I was out of line."

"Me, too. Sorry. I shouldn't have said those things," said Sally.

Eva shrugged—sometimes, it's a gift to be the sullen teenager.

In the small salon they sat in pink swivel chairs. Sally and Eva put their feet in tubs of rumbling water while Julia's face was steamed and smeared with clay by the owner.

Then they were left alone.

"Is that why you stopped making art, Julia?" Sally spoke gently now. "Because of all you went through after Ellis?"

"Truthfully? I didn't want to live like my mom, struggling paycheck to paycheck. I wanted to be comfortable. I like nice things. My painting was never going to get me there. Turns out, I have a much better head for business than I ever did for art."

"I make art," Sally said slowly, "because it's a way of being in this world, of straddling what's out there and what's in here." She touched her chest. "It makes me look closely at the world, and then go deep in for forms and patterns and meaning to get down what I see."

"I always think I'll get back to it someday," said Julia.

Eva closed her eyes, let the water muscle around her feet.

Sally said, "By the way, Julia. Is your mom seeing anyone?"

"She's still with Carlos. They just bought a condo in Sausalito. Why?"

"Dad's single again," Sally said. "So I was wondering . . ."

"Oh, man! And Mom always liked Phil. Well, too bad."

Eva did a swift calculation of how Julia's mom would've factored into the family if she ever got together with Phil. Both were her grandparents, but legally Phil was her father, so if Celia married him, she'd legally be her stepmother, which would make Julia, in addition to being her birth mother, her . . . stepsister? *Thank god for Carlos.*

"We have to find Phil someone," Sally said. "He's lonely and wants us to move back home, which is really aimed at me, because this one's off to college."

"Maybe," Eva said.

Julia swiveled her chair to face Eva. "Maybe what?"

"Maybe I'm going to college," she said.

"Of course you're going to college," said Sally.

"And why wouldn't you?" Julia's clay-covered face made her look like a statue.

"Anything could happen," said Eva.

"Like what?" said Julia.

"I don't know. Ellis never made it."

"That's not going to happen to you, sweetie. He had an accident."

"I could have an accident."

"No reason to think you will," said Julia.

"Weird things repeat in families," said Eva.

"Not like that. More like, your dad was good at math, and you are too."

"Maybe." Eva wasn't about to bring up the generational father-killing pregnancies.

The pedicurists returned. Eva got the blond receptionist and Sally got the napkin folder. Eva had never had a pedicure before and when the receptionist began poking her toes with a sharp metal instrument, she wasn't sure she liked it. She did enjoy the foot massage, and how her nails ended up a shiny, pale shell pink.

In the car, nobody said anything until they were back on the main road to town.

"I'm glad we didn't leave El in that place." Eva patted the box.

"Yeah," said Sally. "And I was feeling guilty about scattering him without Dad and Katie."

"Me, too," said Eva.

Julia pulled up next to Sally's truck in Johnnie's parking lot. "I have an idea," she said. "Let's find a date that's good with everyone and go to Four Mile Beach. That's where Ellis and I met. On hot days up here, we'd go there because it was never crowded, and we could bring the dogs." She must have seen something in Eva's face. "Is that okay with you, sweetheart?"

"I guess." The ocean, at least, was reassuringly eternal. "But I was thinking I'd take him with me."

"Take him where?"

"Ellis never got to go to college, so I thought he could come with me. Wherever I end up. For a while, at least. Then maybe we can go to your beach."

Eva and Wally broke up prom night; he'd expected big things after the dance, and she wouldn't deliver. Later, she heard he found a new girlfriend at Yale, hopefully one more obliging.

Eva went to Pomona. She had a second-floor single in Gibson Hall, with tall windows overlooking a grassy quad and massive white-limbed sycamores. Ellis sat on a bookshelf high up, with a good view outside and her desk right below. She talked to him a lot at first, as if to a roommate. Then she met people, made friends, and grew busy with classes. Days went by when she forgot he was there.

She went home every few weeks, often bringing a friend or two. Sally fed them well. Sometimes Sally and their dad, singly or together, would drive to Claremont and take a few of them out to dinner.

Sally and Charlie dragged along for another seven months, till just before Thanksgiving, when he finally broke it off—still over her calves! "I don't know what it means," he told Sally, "but I need to find out."

Between Christmas and New Year's, all four of the now-single Samuelsons drove north to meet Julia at Four Mile Beach, a pebbly cove off Highway 1. There, on a gray, chilly afternoon, Sally tore off that thick ivory paper and purple ribbon and broke through the yellowed tape on the box's lid. Each person scooped a cupped handful of Ellis's gritty ashes into the surging tide. Then Eva took the box and waded in, the freezing water wicking up her jeans, and she shook out the last of Ellis, her father, her brother, the stranger who made her, and let the box fill up and sink. She stood as the tide pushed and pulled at her legs. The pale late-afternoon sun was on its long slow slide into the ocean. The box knocked against her shins once, twice, then was sucked out to the breakers. With her sneakers full of wet sand, she turned and joined her family on the beach.

The Long Game

There was a time a few years after grad school when Sally Samuelson lived by herself in a cheap little rented house on the north fork of the Fig River. From her kitchen window, she watched lizards do push-ups on a rail fence, while beyond them the land sloped into the dry rocky foothills of the southern Sierras. The closest town, such as it was, was Ingalls, population 350, eight miles away. Sally was there because of love—why else would a single twenty-eight-year-old textile artist exile herself to a dusty backwater?

To support herself, she sewed custom blinds and drapes. She'd come to Ingalls to make window treatments for the Haders' new house (and put some time and distance on a recent breakup). Ruth and Buck Hader were successful artists—and mentors—who'd bought a ranch ten miles up the Bluewater Road. For the three-month job, Sally had set up in Ruth's just-built painting studio, hauling in bolts of fabric, a sewing machine, serger, and commercial iron. She slept on the studio's narrow, built-in daybed and cooked canned soup and beans (the Ingalls general store mostly sold camping supplies) on a hot plate. A mini-fridge hummed to her all night long.

She'd arrived in March, the beginning of spring, when construction on the Haders' new home was in its final stages. At night, she had all thirty acres to herself and soaked naked in the redwood hot tub under the Milky Way, which here in the country was a dense, sky-spanning smear of stars. During the day, a steady stream of subs came to finish the plumbing, the painting, the cabinetry, the stonework. One evening, after merrily drinking boilermakers with some of the workmen, Sally fell into bed with the stonemason, a dark, laconic, intense man whose embrace had surprised and flattered her. She kept sleeping with him night after night, and though neither of them wanted to fall in love—at least not now or here or with each other—that is what happened.

At eleven every morning, Sally took a break from sewing and drove into Ingalls to get her mail at the post office (general delivery), after which she bought herself a coffee and a glazed doughnut. No sign announced the Ingalls doughnut shop, just *Donuts* crookedly spray-stenciled in baby blue on the storefront window. Peering into that window, passersby would see a glass case, empty but for three marvels on the top shelf: a yellowed mountain lion skull and two hairballs, one handball-size in russet red; the other softball-size in salt and pepper—these came from the stomachs of steers, red angus and Holstein respectively.

The shop owners were Opal and Pete Frazier, who had retired early from the gas company. They arrived at four a.m. and opened for business at six every day but Monday. Pete, a fit sixty with snowy white hair and a deep tan, was sweet-tempered and loved by all. He stayed in the back frying and frosting while the haughty and terrifying Opal, ten years Pete's junior, made coffee, served the customers, and manned the register. Short and plump, she scraped her hair back severely and coiled it on the top of her head. At noon, the couple cracked their first beers, and at two, they closed the shop and went home to their double-wide on three weedy acres overlooking the reservoir. Opal told Sally they each drank a case of beer a day. Bud Light for Opal, Bud regular for Pete.

The shop's seating area had old electrical cable spools for tables (obtained for free through Pete's connections at the DWP) and the cheap white plastic chairs sold at supermarkets. For decor, a mounted wild boar's head was looped with tiny red Christmas balls now furred with spiderwebs and dust. A cigarette dangled between tooth and tusk.

Only in such a remote small town, with no competition in sight, could two alcoholic retired civil servants make a go of such a low-energy, minimal business.

The doughnuts, made from commercial mixes, were not bad. Fresh. Generously frosted. Pete had a good touch.

Sally's daily raised glazed was a large, lofty doughnut of unsweetened yeasted dough with a thin, sweet filigree of icing. After a hundred raised glazes, she could have told the weather by this doughnut: On rainy, low-pressure days, they were squatter, denser, the glaze disappointingly moist. On hot spring days, she couldn't open her mouth wide enough to take a real bite and had to nibble her way in while the glaze sent sharp little flakes down her front. How she loved the delicate shatter in each bite!

The north fork of the Fig River—now at high gush in the late spring—ran from the mountains into oak-studded grasslands. It ran through the Haders' ranch and along the old Griffin place that Sally had rented. The stones in the Fig were quartz-veined granite smoothed over centuries into rounded spheres and oblongs. Sally loved granite and quartz—as a girl, she'd had rock collections—so maybe it was not odd that she'd fall for a stonemason. She could watch him work for hours. He was not tall, but strong and balanced, and careful in his movements. He'd take ten minutes selecting a rock, then heft and spin and study it before nestling it into place. The Haders' massive fireplace, made of blobby, gradated white river rocks, had a subtle cartoonish humor; for the pillars flanking their gate on the Bluewater Road the stonemason used darker, rounder, speckled rocks for a more restrained, even formal look.

Balance, precision, emotion expressed in rock.

His hands were porous and rough, and rasped her skin in a pleasurable way.

A standard obstacle sweetened—and hindered—their love: his wife of twenty-three years. Viv. The mother of his kids, two boys and one girl, sixteen to twenty-two years old.

When his work on the Haders' property was almost done, the stonemason said, "I guess I'll have to leave Viv, now, and be with you."

Sally first felt this as a triumph—to beat out a wife of twenty-some years!—and promptly disliked herself for thinking that way. Besides, how could she be competitive with a lumpen forty-four-year-old horsewoman with salon-stiffened, dyed-beige hair? (Sally's hair was fine, dark blond, and long; she wore it in one or two skinny braids.) The stonemason wasn't exactly the brilliant brooding painter or potter she'd pictured for herself, but possibly an improvement: a brooding, skilled craftsman. But . . . would they have to stay up here? Maybe, like the Haders, they could come and go. Town and country. She imagined a mountain home built of river stone. Garden walls of stone and clinker brick. A getaway. "Yes," she told the stonemason. "Let's do it."

As it happened, Viv wasn't so easily shaken. She demanded that the stonemason give their marriage one more try. "I guess I owe her that," he said. "If only to prove once and for all that the marriage is dead. And has been dead for years."

Sally wondered if Viv—who, according to the stonemason, did most of the child-rearing, cooked the meals, and kept the house—had any idea that the marriage was dead.

"I'll be in Pasadena," Sally said. She lived in a bungalow court with her younger sister, who now was mostly away at college. "I'm easy to find."

The stonemason's expression turned darker. "I couldn't bear that," he said. "I need you nearby. Can't you give me the summer?"

He even knew of a house she could rent on the river and gave her the number to call. As luck would have it—she took it as a sign—the ceramics teacher out at the junior college got sick, and the Haders, who knew the sick man, suggested that Sally, a ceramics minor in undergrad, could finish his classes through June. Ruth Hader said if Sally could stand to stick around a few more months, she could probably teach his summer school classes as well. "It would look good on your résumé," Ruth said, "and as I know almost nobody up here, having you around would be wonderful. We can walk."

They walked early, in the coolness at six thirty a.m., Mondays, Wednesdays, and Fridays, taking fire roads into the hills, or the fisherman's path along the Fig. Sally said nothing about the stonemason to long-married and motherly Ruth Hader, who, from the allusions she made to Buck's youthful antics, might not look kindly on adultery.

By eight thirty, Sally was on her way to the junior college where she taught weekdays till noon. She now hit the doughnut shop on her way home. She'd grown friendly with ill-tempered Opal. Sally was adept with difficult people—her own mother had been very difficult, as was Buck Hader, and the stonemason. Surly, moody people needed the easygoing, she reasoned: Who else could get along with them?

Opal, like Sally, was a big reader. She and Sally swapped novels. Opal gave her *Lonesome Dove*. She gave Opal *The Tin Drum*.

The big rush at the doughnut shop ran from six thirty till eight and was mostly men. Men on their way to work. Men stopping in to talk to other men and caffeinate. By the time Sally came in, business was intermittent and Opal was free to chat.

"Isn't he a famous actor?" A female customer swung her chin to indicate a black-haired, bearded man holding court at a spool table.

"That asshole?" Opal said.

Sally recognized the county building inspector from his visit to the Haders' place. He did look like a Hollywood frontiersman today, all fringed up: fringed leather vest, fringed knee-high mocs, fringed leather pouch slung on a wide, yes, fringed strap.

The building inspector, seeing the three women looking at him, waved and smiled. Teeth alarmingly white. Beard precision-cut.

"He's in the movies, right?" the customer hissed.

"One movie," Opal said. "Straight to video. A boring piece of shit."

Opal's churlish doughnut shop persona had at first intimidated Sally, but she now found it hilarious.

"Ima get his autograph." The woman took a small crisp paper napkin and went over.

Sally said to Opal, "So what's with the Davy Crockett look?"

"He's a mountain man reenactor. They go out in the woods, clean their muskets, smoke corncob pipes. Track bunnies."

The two women laughed.

Sally had asked the stonemason what giving his marriage a last try meant for the two of them. He said, "Can't say yet. I suppose I shouldn't see you for a while."

"What is a while? A week? A month? All summer?"

"Can't say yet."

"So there's a chance that even if I'm here, I might not see you all summer?"

"I doubt it will be as long as that."

She never thought she'd love a married master craftsperson in the boonies. He lived up here, he said, because he liked the room, the hills, the fishing and hiking, and because his wife had horses—Missouri Fox Trotters—which was where all her interest and energy were concentrated, with none left for him, not for years.

He and Viv, he said, had nothing in common except for the kids. Two were already out of the house. The youngest was graduating high school next June.

He'd been lonely. And then came Sally with her soulful laugh and bright eyes and warm, open face. So smart and funny, if not particularly pretty. He said that. *Not particularly pretty.* He swore, though, that he loved her looks.

But twenty-three years ago he'd made a solemn vow and he owed Viv a last try to uphold it. Did he want to try? No. But vows existed to override passing impulses and emotions. Were his emotions passing? He thought not, but they'd find out.

He brought her a tiny black kitten from a litter abandoned at the sawmill. Female. He brought bowls and a sack of kitten chow. "So you won't be alone here."

Sally named her Millie. After the sawmill.

She was now paying for two places, here on the Fig and the courtyard cottage in Pasadena she had long shared with her sister Eva. She and Eva talked every night on the telephone. After a year of dorm life in Claremont, Eva was happy to have the cottage to herself, though she did miss Sally.

Here, as in Pasadena, Sally sewed napkins and place mats to sell at local weekend craft shows, which she found in the valley towns of Fresno, Visalia, Porterville. She also sewed stuffed toys that, she acknowledged, were potentially frightening to children. (She liked to think of future adults being haunted by strange, emotionally charged images whose origins they could not quite place.) Her goods competed against a tidal wave of the local fabric art that she dubbed "pufferware": quilted padded covers for photo albums, Kleenex boxes, toilet seat lids, toasters, teapots, phone books, whatever could be covered. The chosen yardage was usually gingham, but some fabricators used quilting calicos in tiny florals; all added ruffled lace edging. Sally could make a mint if she succumbed to this craze, but she could not. She could not. A few tea cozies in Indian block prints and some felted wool glasses cases were the closest she came to covering anything, and even these items proved too severe for the pufferware crowd, and too expensive. She'd done far better at her craft fairs down south, where she used to live. Where her sister and friends and other family members still lived. Where solid colors, nubbly linen, and elegant simplicity sold well.

Pete and I were wondering. Good-looking, smart, funny woman like you. Surely there's a boyfriend?" Opal poured Sally coffee as she spoke. "Or girlfriend?"

"Boyfriend. Sort of," said Sally. "Though he doesn't think I'm good-looking."

"Dump the bastard," said Opal. "Pete and I think you're darling."

"Oh. Thanks."

"Is he down south or up here?"

"Here."

"Does he have a name?"

"Can't say," Sally replied. "Not yet." She hardly ever said the stonemason's name anyway because she hated it. She couldn't believe that such a serious, smoldering, skilled man would share a name with cartoon pilots, ersatz aristocrats, and banquet-size cuts of beef. Baron. The Red Baron. Baron von Richthofen. Baron of beef.

Worse yet, he'd answer to the nickname. Barney.

She called him *You*. You want more coffee? You want to sleep here? In bed, she said, *You, you, you.*

When necessary—so, almost never—she called him Barn. Barn was almost okay, if you didn't think of a big space full of machinery, hay, and shitting livestock.

It had been twenty-two days with no word from the stonemason, and agitation made her reckless. "He's married," she blurted to Opal. "My boyfriend."

"I guessed as much. Pete was married when we met."

Sally's heart leapt with hope. "He's giving his marriage one last go. To prove to his wife that it's over."

Opal tightened her bun, refixed a few pins. Sometimes, as now, she looked quite severe. "That sounds, uh— Yes?"

An elderly man—not a local—was asking for a spoon.

"Coffee stirrers are there." Opal pointed to the cream-and-sugar station.

The man went back to his wife, a slight, gray-haired woman hunched over her coffee cup; half a coconut doughnut sat on a napkin beside it.

Opal turned back to Sally. "If I guess who it is, will you tell me?"

"That's the thing!" cried Sally. "If word gets back to him that I blabbed—"

"I'm sorry . . ." The spoon-seeking man was back. "My wife really needs a *spoon* spoon," he said, and lowered his voice. "She likes to sup her coffee."

Opal, in her coldest voice, said, "No spoons, sorry."

"Surely there's a spoon in the back somewhere."

"Surely, there is not," said Opal.

Sally wished she had the nerve to be so steely.

The man huffed and spoke to his wife. The two left, the woman holding her half a doughnut high as if dogs were snapping at it.

Opal said to Sally, "Of course we have spoons. But who wants to watch some old gal suh-up her coffee? Disgusting!"

The two women laughed. Sally climbed off the stool. "Gotta go," she said. "Gotta finish a batch of napkins for tomorrow's fair."

At five weeks—thirty-five days—and still no word from the stonemason, Sally's need to talk about him, to conjure him with words, eclipsed her discretion. Plus, she craved information, and after ten years at the cash register of the doughnut shop, Opal was a fount. "Okay, you can guess who I'm seeing."

Opal guessed the building inspector.

"Are you kidding? He's too vain. And silly."

"Bill? He's actually a good guy."

"You said he was an asshole."

"He is. But he's all right. He takes good care of his wife."

"Why, what's wrong with her?"

"Rheumatoid arthritis, rapidly progressing."

"I've never actually talked to him," Sally said. "No. My guy's a stonemason."

"Not Barney Reese?" said Opal. "We're practically related. His sister's married to Pete's son. Gosh. Barney? I'd never put you two together. He's so grouchy."

Grouchy! Sally delighted in the word. The stonemason *was* grouchy.

"I like 'em sunny, like Pete," Opal went on. "I'm too grouchy myself."

"I must like 'em grouchy," Sally said. "I like you."

"It's not just that he's grouchy. I don't know. . . . He's so . . . so . . ." It was one thirty in the afternoon and Opal wasn't quite slurring, but getting there. "So *unto himself.*"

That's exactly what drew Sally to him. *So unto himself.* When he first took her in his arms, it was as if she'd entered a large, cool, secret room.

Sally had just planted a six-pack of Early Girls when she heard his truck. She was coiling a hose on the side of the house. She checked herself—cutoffs, a tank top; she hadn't braided her hair today and it hung in strings around her face. Her heart commenced a crazy tom-tom. Was this it? Had he come to say he was giving her up? Or that their life together could begin? Around her, the yellow pastures and blue Sierras pulsed and swirled. She must collect herself. If she looked too pleased, it might scare him off. Casual, unhurried, she rounded the corner of the house.

That was not the stonemason's trim blue Ranger but a gray Chevy double cab bustled with toolboxes. And there, at her gate, in all his clichéd cinematic beauty, was the building inspector. Unfringed. Khakis and an olive-green work shirt. "Up this way," he said. "Heard someone moved into Griffin's old place, so I came to see who."

"Me," she said.

"Bill Woodrow," he said.

"I know," she said. "The building inspector. Sally Samuelson."

"I know," he said. "Opal says you're a seamstress."

"Opal shouldn't talk about people."

"You tell her that," he said. And they laughed.

She kept the fence—waist-high white rails stapled with hog wire—between them. They talked tomatoes: how often to water them, whether to sucker them (he did, she didn't), the pesty spider mites and hornworms. Good manners and neighborliness suggested she offer him coffee or cold water. She did not.

His kids were in college back east, the girl at Michigan, the boy at Penn State. But both coming home for the summer. He looked at his watch. "I got to be in Visalia by four, so, nice to meet you, Sally Samuelson."

Putting away the hoe and shovel, Sally thought that the building inspector was too confident. Too upbeat. He lacked the deep soundings of psychic pain that called to her. The lingering traces of some old damage, never extirpated.

He was, in every way, not the stonemason.

Who showed up that very night, late. She had Joni on and hadn't heard his truck; he walked in calling her name and seized hold of her. He'd been drinking. They tumbled into bed. "You," she said to him. "You, you, you."

"I shouldn't be here," he said. "But it's killing me."

"It's killing me, too."

Before he left, they sat at the kitchen table, and each drank a finger of bourbon. She had many questions, but she didn't want to pressure him, lest she run him off. "Today the building inspector stopped by to see who lived here," she said.

"Woodrow's a good guy. Fair." The stonemason looked more closely at her. "Why was he here?"

"To see who'd moved in."

The stonemason brooded over his whiskey. "You got to hold fast, Sally," he said. "Hold fast. Don't let me go."

The information she extracted from Opal was not promising. Opal had never noticed storm clouds in the stonemason's marriage. She'd seen them at a family barbecue just last week. Nothing appeared out of whack. "He'd made a salsa he was proud of. Made everybody taste it," said Opal. "Needed salt."

Nothing Opal said, and not the long empty days when he did not call or come by, tempered Sally's longing. Abandoning discretion and caution, she confessed all to Ruth Hader, who said, "The guy that did our stonework? Him? Huh. Isn't he married? He is? Huh. Has he ever even been to an art museum?"

All through July and most of August, Sally longed. She yearned. She waited. She sat still at her sewing machine, gazing at the dark fringe of oaks along the Fig River. She was teetering on a narrow ledge, she thought, and a single word could topple her into misery. Or bliss.

The building inspector entered with his son and daughter, both tall and abnormally good-looking, and his wife, who, while clearly fragile and ill—pale and curling into herself—was still a beauty. A dying small-town queen. They moved through the tables greeting people, touching shoulders, clasping hands, then settled around the spool beneath the boar's head. The building inspector brought Opal their order. While she pulled doughnuts from the glass case, he turned to Sally. "Tomatoes flowering yet?" Later, on his way out, he introduced Sally to his family. "She's in the old Griffin place," he said.

"Then you have the best swimming hole," said his daughter.

"Come swimming," Sally said. "Anytime."

"John Griffin and I killed four rattlesnakes in one day in your yard," said his son.

"I wish you'd come kill some more," Sally said.

"Lovely to meet you, Sally," said the wife. Her voice was still strong.

"Likewise," Sally said. "Lovely."

The next time the building inspector stopped by her house, it was the same thing: she heard a truck and her heart boomed in panic, her hands shook, fate loomed ominously, and then it was only the building inspector. They chatted outside. What did she do out here all by herself? Sewed. And read. He read too, the classics. Dickens and Trollope were his favorites. He belonged to a Trollope club and once a year, he said, "there's a big get-together. A conference. With a Trollope trivia contest."

"Here's a question," she said. "If your mountain-man reenactment weekend coincided with your Trollope conference, which would you choose?"

"That's a tough one," he said. "Both are just a heckuva lot of fun."

"I've never read Trollope," said Sally.

"Oh—Opal passed on your *Tin Drum* to me," he said. "I hope you don't mind."

So they were a kind of three-way book club now.

Bill Woodrow's got his eye on you."

"Not like that."

"Of course like that."

"He's never made any kind of move."

"Bill takes his time," Opal said. "He's waiting for a sign."

"He won't get one from me."

"He's very patient. He plays a long game. He waited four years for my friend Abigail."

"And what happened there?"

"They had a lovely time, but he wouldn't leave his wife."

"Just because I love a married man doesn't mean I have a thing for them."

In fact, now that she knew the powerlessness of loving someone married, she would never, not ever, put herself in that position again. As for the building inspector, she would never be someone's latest auxiliary interest, ranked somewhere between Trollope and mountain-manhood. Nobody would ever call her a heckuva lot of fun.

They watched her tomatoes grow and fruit. He admired her cookie sheets of halved oblong Romas drying in the sun.

Once, in a late-summer heatwave, they walked down to the river to see how low the swimming hole was. The Fig, so boisterous and foamy in the spring, had become a narrow, sluggish tea-colored trickle. In the white slab rocks, stranded pools of water had turned a bright, pretty algae green. She and the building inspector sat on the log where she usually left her towel and clothes. She kept a chaste distance from him. They watched two reddish-brown snakes swimming side by side in synchronized curls.

"I'm never swimming here again," she said.

"They won't hurt you," he said.

She wanted to ask him about the stonemason. The two men knew each other. She might learn something. For whatever reason—discretion, shyness, embarrassment—she couldn't bring herself to do it.

She never once invited the building inspector inside her home.

Summer school would be over in a week. The community college had asked her to teach ceramics and textile design in the fall. Her sister was lonely and eager for her to come home for the last few weeks of summer. She had to decide by the following Monday. Really, her answer depended on the stonemason—should she keep waiting?

Ruth Hader said she'd waited too long already. "If he wants you, he'll find you."

Opal said her odds weren't good. "Even lousy marriages can have deep roots."

The stonemason himself showed up Saturday morning. He couldn't stay long. He had bags of groceries, perishables, in his truck and a keg of beer—all was for his middle son's twenty-first birthday party. But he had to see her. He missed her. He loved her. It soothed and inspired him to have her nearby.

After they messed up her bed, she asked how his life was at home.

"As it's always been. She does her thing, I do mine."

"She's still happy with you?"

"Seems so."

"And you?"

"Happy? No." He swung his legs out of bed. "We married very young, before we knew each other. If I met her now, I'd never be interested."

Impatience overruled her usual reticence. "So do you think you'll leave her?"

He stood up and gathered his clothes, annoyed. "As you know, Sally, I'm working on it." He sat on the bed to pull on his jeans. "But it'll kill her," he said. "I want to leave, yes. I just need more time to figure out how."

"It's been five months."

He stood and hitched his jeans and glowered down at her. "Well, I can't do it today, what with all my kids home for the party."

Opal and Pete invited her to dinner that Sunday, a first. They moved with the slow, wavery deliberateness of drunks, but managed to produce a yellow rice dish with almonds and raisins, a fresh green salad, and a plump roasted chicken.

After eating, they moved with new beers into the trailer's tiny living room. Opal suggested they watch a movie. A dirty movie. Triple-X.

Just because I'm in love with a married man, Sally thought, *ev-*

eryone thinks I'm a libertine. "Oh, no thanks," she said. "That's all right."

"You know, Pete and I would love a three-way. If you're inclined . . ."

"I'm actually kind of a prude," Sally said.

They took her refusal lightly but seemed surprised. "Can't blame us for trying," said Opal.

Driving home, Sally was creeped out. Shocked. She'd thought they were friends, like all her friends, but they had quite a different idea. Too different for her to reconcile. Sally wished she was driving home not to the ugly little rental on the Fig, but to her pretty Craftsman cottage and beloved sister in the Pasadena bungalow court.

Yes. She'd go back. Let the stonemason find her there.

She might have driven south right then, but she'd paid for a booth at the Visalia craft fair next weekend; plus, she had grades to turn in, and office hour appointments with a couple of students who wanted to be artists, the poor things. She intended to discourage them.

She was hemming place mats when a bobcat—those telltale tufted ears—sauntered across the pasture toward the river. She ran outside and called for her cat—"Millie, kitty, kitty, kitty, kitty, kitty-kitty." She pushed through the gate and dashed around the side of the barn and there, behind the barn, dirt gave way underfoot; one foot broke through the crust, and when she lunged to step forward, the ground there also gave in, and in a crashing of dirt and rotten, splintering, papery wood, she dropped down. This happened fast, but her thoughts slowed to make sense of it and her mind, at some remove, narrated: *She fell into a well.*

Her left foot hit with a knuckly crunch, a white explosion of pain.

After a minute or ten—who could tell?—she struggled to sit up, legs straight out in front of her. Her heart and breathing slowed and her eyes adjusted to the dimness of the small earthen chamber. Above, a gash of sky with splintered edges. Below, one ankle flopped at a sickening angle. Nausea's warm salty saliva filled her mouth. Best not to move. Moving triggered electrical currents of pure, obliterative pain. She panted. She stayed still and took stock. She was maybe nine, ten feet down.

The hole was too large for a well. Too large and deep for a grave. A roughly rectangular pit, it was too long in both dimensions to brace her good leg against one wall and shinny up. The earthen sides bulged with rocks.

Please don't be an old outhouse, she whimper-thought.

Her ankle throbbed, but that was nothing compared to when she moved it. Her heart pounded. She wouldn't die here, she told herself sternly. She'd claw her way up. Or she'd claw down one wall to make a slope she could crawl up. Even if it took days. She was well fed. The nights were still warm. She could live for days.

Millie, silhouetted against the bright sky, peered down at her.

She wept, then, from fear, and pain, and months of accumulated loneliness. A snotty, painful-in-the-throat weeping.

Maybe she couldn't get out. Nobody ever walked around the old barn on this property. Not even she, who lived here, had—or she'd have fallen through months ago. Nobody would find her because nobody would miss her. Tuesday, Opal might notice that she hadn't come in for her daily raised glazed, but she and Pete would think their proposition had insulted her—and it had! Ruth Hader would be annoyed that she didn't show up for their Wednesday morning walk, but would she come looking?

Sally palmed the closest protuberant rocks and tried to wiggle them. Nothing budged. So climbing out seemed possible, if she could manage on one foot. She'd done some rock climbing with an old boyfriend, but never got the bug or really understood the allure. And she'd never climbed with only one good foot.

She wept again. For ending up in a dirt pit. For ending up in Ingalls. Down here, the stonemason didn't seem real. Her mind slid off him. Had she ever felt anything true for him? Or just this new, needling anger? She had to get out of here, here being this pit, the shoddy rental, and Ingalls, with its grimy doughnut shop and an entanglement she never should have allowed. If she got out, she was done. Done with the stonemason, done with these rocky, dry foothills, all of it. She breathed in hoarse sobs, into which soon bled a familiar sound: a truck, at least eight cylinders loud, coming up the drive. Crunching to a stop in the gravel parking area. The engine switched off; the radio, loud, emitted symphonic Beethoven-ish measures and went silent. A door opened.

Sally screamed at the top of her lungs.

The building inspector drove her to the ER in Porterville. "A bomb shelter," he said. John Griffin Sr. had started to dig it but gave up once Kennedy stared down Khrushchev. That had to be, what, 1962? No wonder the plywood covering had rotted.

He had lowered a ladder into the pit and very carefully carried her out on his broad, surprisingly warm back.

She will never forget that back.

He stayed, too, as she was x-rayed and had her bone set. While they waited for the nurse who would put on her cast, he said he had to return his work truck and check in at the county office. He could be back in two hours, or he could call someone to come get her. He checked his watch. "Maybe not Pete and Opal," he said. "They'll be too deep in their cups to drive."

"Call Baron Reese," she said.

"Barney? Really? Okay." A flicker of puzzlement, and the building inspector went down the hall to call. He returned in a minute. "He's sorry, but he can't get away."

It was the Haders, then, who came and took her to their beautiful new home, put her on the sofa in front of the blobby stone fireplace, and fed her dinner. "High time you ended your little romance with the rustics," Ruth Hader said, covering Sally with a quilt. "Time for you to class up."

It was a truly magnificent fireplace.

Sally left Ingalls, the ugly little cottage, the nearly dry Fig River, the doughnut shop, her pufferware competition, and the decent teaching job. She went back to where she came from, to her sister Eva, the bungalow court, her old friends and usual craft fairs, her connections in the art world, and the custom-blind business.

She never spoke to the stonemason after the day of his son's twenty-first birthday party.

"All for the best," Ruth Hader said.

Twenty-odd years later and long married to a painting professor, Sally Samuelson (she kept her own name) sometimes wakes in the morning to a distinct feeling—not quite a memory, more a glimmer, a whiff of her time in Ingalls. This has nothing to do with the stonemason, whom she now regards, with a pinch of shame, as a regrettable ethical lapse. She has never gone back there—she refused so many invitations from the Haders, they long ago stopped asking her.

The first time she had this feeling was maybe three years after she left. A slight tug in the air, a faint, general brightening.

For some reason, she thought of the building inspector. Two days later, she was walking around the Rose Bowl with Ruth Hader, who said she'd just seen the building inspector in Ingalls, at the new little market there. "His wife died last year. Oh, and he asked about you," Ruth said. "I told him you'd married a wonderful guy. He smiled, but his eyes looked sad—of course, there's a general sadness about him now. He says hello and that he's happy for you."

A coincidence. But the feeling—the tiny tug, the shimmering brightened air, the sense of him—has returned at odd moments.

As Opal had said, the building inspector was patient. It would seem the game he began is not yet up. Sally can tell when she's on his mind. Today, she smiles and looks at her sleeping husband. She has never told him of the building inspector, not even that he saved her life. She keeps this brief brightening, this rare, faint wash of love, as her own small secret. Hardly worth mentioning. Ever treasured.

23andJP

JP Durand was thirty-three years old and an assistant professor of pure and applied mathematics at the University of California, San Diego, when he found out that his father—that big wheezy elephant Claude Durand (1919–2007), who had built skyscrapers from Boston to Jakarta and had a nose like a pyramid and snow-white eyebrows that, like head hair, never stopped growing; Claude, who had roared and blustered and beguiled everyone he met—was not, in fact, his biological father.

JP's wife, Pilar, had given him a 23andMe DNA test kit for Christmas. She'd already taken her test and was impressed, even delighted, by her ancestry: Western European, Mesoamerican, and Afro-Cuban, mostly. Three continents!

When his results came back via email, he waited to look at them at home with Pilar. She nestled against him on the sofa, the laptop on their knees. "They won't be as colorful as mine," she said.

JP first had to register on the site, but finally, he clicked through the links to "Ancestry Composition," where the very first line was "Ashkenazi Jewish 50%."

"Son of a gun!" JP instantly assumed one parent had hidden their heritage.

Pilar then reached over and clicked to the "DNA Relatives" page, where the first entries included two half sisters and a half niece, two with the last name of Samuelson, one Yu. JP had never heard of them.

"Traviesa Yvette," said Pilar. Naughty Yvette.

Pilar was quick. She understood before he did.

One of JP's first thoughts was, *Well, that makes sense.*

All his life, people said he was his mother's son, because he was slim and small and dark like her, and because he looked nothing like Claude. His brother, François, on the other hand, was a Claude clone.

And then came a salty taste in his mouth. A wobble in his balance as he stood.

"I'm so sorry, mi amor," Pilar said. "I had no idea."

Of course, he didn't sleep that night. A massive recalibration was underway. Pilar held him and sometimes murmured as he lay open-eyed in the dark.

"I knew there was something that I liked about you," she

said. "Almost all my old boyfriends were Jewish, starting with Sammy when I was thirteen. It was great—I got to go to all the bar and bat mitzvahs that year. Seemed like every other weekend. And I went to shabbat dinners, my first Passover seder."

"Then you know more about all that than I do," said JP.

They had married two years before, after knowing each other barely six months; they'd rushed the wedding and held it in Oaxaca so Claude could be there. He'd died three weeks later. They'd hurried back from Bali to hold his hand in those last days.

Now, with this rude correction, JP had lost Claude all over again. Again, he mourned that huge, unruly, embarrassing, and beloved dad, the dad to whom he now had no claim. Memories intruded on repeat: Claude untangling his kite in the Sanam Luang park, Claude urging him to eat magenta-colored ham in Madrid, Claude kissing his head when leaving for work in the morning, Claude pushing and cuffing him up the Monte Albán pyramid, Claude roaring with hilarity and obvious pride while reading aloud incomprehensible sentences in JP's PhD dissertation. Claude pale and ancient and weeping in a wheelchair at his wedding. Claude, his largest, loudest, most exuberant source of love, encouragement, and approval, had been hoaxed.

"Oh, JP, nobody would ever say you weren't Claude's son," Pilar said when he tried to explain this disenfranchisement, his caving sense of loss. "He raised you, that's a fact. Never mind one long-ago sperm."

Yet it was a blow, he insisted, to contain no Claude.
And who was this interloping Ashkenazi?

He googled "23andMe stories," "23andMe surprises," "23and-Me disasters," and in the anonymous comment lines, he found that his situation was not unique. Many—even most—commenters expressed an anger he recognized. A prevalent coarseness, allowed and fueled by anonymity, was somehow gratifying.

> Seems like mom was a real ho while dad was in Nam. Says my bio dad could be one of several.

> Found out my dad's not my bio dad. Showed my mom and (fake) dad my ancestry results and now they aren't speaking to each other. Whatta shitshow!!!

The googling soothed him like a pill, though he came to loathe the term *bio dad*.

> Learned my dad isn't really my dad. Mom was surprised, too—always thought I looked like her husband. Seems bio dad was a kid she met in a bar and had fast drunk sex with while her hubby played pool! Kid's name was Curtis, she thinks.

> My Bio dad was a med student who sold his spunk for cash. I have six half siblings so far—and they're

> just the ones who've ancestry tested. At least my folks picked someone who looked like the man who will always be my "real" dad. I still want to meet the wanking med student.

Artless as these squibs were, they helped him articulate (to himself, at least) what had happened. The tsunami in his life. He wrote some squibs of his own on his phone, as notes to himself. Not that he'd ever post one:

> Learned at almost 34 that my dad wasn't my real dad and my mom has lied to me all my life. My brother is now my half brother, and I have half sisters and a half niece I never knew existed—and a bio dad, who's maybe living, maybe not.

He duly googled the half sisters and niece. Katherine Yu was a psychiatrist in private practice in Brentwood. In her headshot, she did not look Asian; rather, with her dark curly hair, narrow face, and sharply arched eyebrows, she looked like him. The half niece, Eva Samuelson, taught physics—her listed specialty was soft condensed matter—at Harvey Mudd College. She also had the dark hair and narrow face.

At least they were smart.

According to her website, Sally Samuelson was an artist who showed at a gallery in Santa Monica. Photos showed a plain, friendly face and long, skinny, light brown braids, a shin-length full skirt worn with stylish combat boots. Yvette would sniff.

But JP liked the hip, arty look, and her peculiar, gridlike string wall hangings that had words knotted in.

It might help to talk to Yvette," said Pilar.

"Oh, I will," he said. Once the shock and queasiness ebbed. He wanted to gather his wits before his mom took over the narrative. Before she spun her web.

Yvette, at sixty-eight, was still living in Oaxaca and taking on jobs. After Claude died, she'd brought her widowed, ninety-one-year-old mother to live with her. JP and François had been trying to convince the two women to move to California—François had a house with a granny flat in Culver City—but Yvette said she'd stay in her Mexico home as long as she could manage the stairs. Even their grandmother still made it up and down those stairs.

His parents' marriage had been a great mythic structure in JP's life. Grizzled, exuberant Claude and beautiful, strict Yvette. The Queen, Claude called her. The Queen of Sheba. He also said that they—he and Yvette—were "a case of Beauty and the Beast—and she tamed the beast!"

At Claude's memorial, Nonie, JP's half sister—his *former* half sister, now just a stepsister—from Claude's first marriage, had regaled JP with stories of the father she'd known growing up. "When I was a kid, women *swarmed* Claude. They phoned him at home at all hours. They showed up at our door. Some befriended our mom—one even came on vacation with us. Mom got to where she couldn't take it anymore. When she finally kicked him out, Claude was devastated. He refused to believe she was serious. He got himself this awful beige apartment—it was like a Motel 6 room with a hot plate. He didn't bathe or cut his hair or eat for, like, two years. He thought Mom would take pity on him. She didn't. But a lot of other women did. Every time Charlotte and I went over there, some new woman was cooking soup on the hot plate—young, his age, older, he was an equal-opportunity womanizer. This went on till Yvette. He was completely different with her. Crazy about her. She laid down the law and he cleaned himself up. He got rid of all the other women and that was that. As he liked to say, she tamed the beast."

But who tamed her?

On impulse, as he drove home from a day of teaching, he speed-dialed his mother on the free long-distance app they used.

"Allo," she said, in her usual French way. "Is that you, JP?"

"Hi, Mom, I'm calling because I got some news."

"Is Pilar—?"

"No, Mom. Not that." They had told her they were planning to start a family and now every call began with disappointing her. "This is about me. And you. And some guy named Samuelson."

He drove a full block in her silence. "Who?" Or maybe it was, "Oh?"

"Pilar gave me a 23andMe test for Christmas. That's a DNA test, Mom. I finally took it. And guess what it said."

The line crackled until he was sure they'd been cut off. "You there?"

"Oh, JP. I really didn't know." Her voice trembled.

"What do you mean you didn't know? You had no idea?"

"I wondered, maybe, at first . . . but by the time you were born, you could only have been Claude's. Although later, I sometimes thought . . ."

He pulled over to the curb a few blocks from their condo to stabilize the connection. The ocean air was bright with light afternoon mist. The hedges and bushes in nearby yards were thick and ragged with new growth. "Come on, Mom. Did you know or not?"

"I swear, JP. No. Sometimes I suspected. I was never sure."

During her pregnancy, she said, she had worried, but then JP was born so long after Phil—*Phil!*—left Saudi Arabia, it seemed impossible that he was the father. "You were born almost forty-four weeks after Phil left. Ten thousand times I counted those weeks!"

A seagull lazed over the street so low, JP saw the orange dot on its yellow beak. "So—who is this *Phil*?"

"Phil?" He sensed her gathering up her story, giving it a swift shaping and edit. "Gosh, JP. Such a long time ago. I hardly remember. He was Claude's project supervisor in Saudi. Someone headquarters sent out," she said. "But Claude kept getting called to Jeddah, so the two of us—Phil and I—we had a lot of time together."

JP had to understand, she raced on in her rapid, lightly accented English, how lonely she'd been in the awful, claustrophobic Aramco camp. Not allowed to work. Stuck at home with a toddler. The other mothers ignorant, racist, and silly. Claude gone for days at a stretch. "That was the only time your father and I were not completely happy together."

JP could think of a few other times. Their marriage had had its weather.

"I was desperate for adult company. Phil was easy to talk to. And kind. We drank too much; everyone did in that terrible place. And Phil was good-natured. I mean, he was nobody special, just a company engineer, but very modest and sweet and low-key—not at all like your father."

"Except he is my father, Mom. Phil is my father."

"No. You know what I mean."

A spiky blackness lapped at the edges of his eyes. "I have to go now, Mom," he said. "Talk soon. Bye."

When she phoned back an hour later, he was home on his exercise bike, seven furious miles in. He picked up and she was talking and clanking dishes in a sink.

"So you know, JP, forty-three, forty-four weeks would have meant a freakishly long, very late-term pregnancy," she said.

"And you were perfectly normal. The doctor assured me you were a perfect, full-term baby. And believe me, JP, I asked. Many times."

"Someone got their facts wrong."

"You don't know this yet, JP, but you will soon enough, so I'll speak frankly: Babies are born covered in a white, yogurt-like substance—sorry to be so explicit, but you'll see it soon enough when Pilar gives birth. . . . But by forty-two, forty-three weeks, there is no white stuff. It has been reabsorbed. Late-term babies are born dry and big and often with complications. I've heard this from several doctors. But you were not born dry, and you were not big, and the birth was not difficult. You came out all-around average—an average juicy normal little thing," she said.

"Okay, Mom." He needed her to stop with the obstetrical. And the average bit—who wants to be average? "I get it."

Since Saudi, she rushed on, she'd run into Phil once, in California, "when I was checking out Thacher school for you. A total coincidence. But when he laughed, it was exactly your laugh. That got me wondering all over again."

Pilar said JP laughed like a machine gun. *Uh-uh-uh-uh-uh-uh-uh-uh-uh-uh-uh.*

"Maybe I should have pursued it then," she said. "But that was twenty years ago, and at the time, Claude wasn't doing well. He'd just had heart surgery, right after prostate cancer. I thought, why poison his last days? Who knew he'd live eighteen more years? A few times, I thought of saying something to you, but what did I have to go on? A three-second laugh? I suppose I might have asked Phil to take a paternity test. But why? To drop a bomb on two families? And anyway, JP, Claude *was* your father. He raised you. He supported you. He worshipped your intelligence. You couldn't have had a more loving, loyal, devoted father."

"I know. I get it, Mom." Again, he needed her to stop talking.

"Are you going to contact Phil?" she said. "Will you meet him? He's not that far from you, assuming he's still in Pasadena."

"I've got to go now. We can talk later. Bye, Mom."

Learned that bio dad was my dad's supervisor. Mom and supe drank a little too much and yours truly is the result.

JP googled "Phil Samuelson" and found a LinkedIn listing and a website for Samuelson and Pike Engineering in Altadena. In both, the same small headshot revealed a bland Caucasian face with short, tight gray curls and large brown spaniel eyes.

How to replace his glamorous, towering monument of a father with postage-stamp Phil?

"I found the guy's contact information," he told Pilar. "Phil's."

"Will you cold-call him?"

"If anything, an email. Let him have his first reaction in private."

"You're nice. I'd be dying of curiosity. I am dying of curiosity. If it were me, I'd have already called him and all the sisters, too."

"But what if they're horrible, total weirdos who attach themselves to us and we can't ever get free?"

Pilar, laughing, slid her arms around him. "Isn't that what family is?"

He had a family. A father. It's not as if he'd been raised by a single mother with an aching absence where a father should have been. He didn't need a great void filled. He was curious about this Phil—maybe not as curious as Pilar—but shy. Wary. He was not a social person. He did not meet people easily. He'd grown up with language barriers; whenever they moved to a new country, for the first months, his brother and parents were the only people he talked to—the only people he *could* talk to. Now, he worked in a field where barely a handful of colleagues could talk about his work. His three close friends—one each from high school, Stanford, and Berkeley—he saw maybe once a year. He had never been focused on people.

He'd seen too many of his classmates let their social lives impede their academic progress. After one serious girlfriend in college who demanded more time than he had to give, he'd resolved not to have another until he was tenure track. By the time San Diego hired him, almost everyone he knew was married or at least paired up, and the number of viable single women, infinite in college and somewhat circumscribed in grad school, had dwindled to zero. Only then had it occurred to him that his focus on academics might have impeded his chances for love and a family.

He had been at UCSD for two years when he met Pilar in Oaxaca. He'd been visiting his parents and was reading in a park called the Llano by the high fountain, whose mist cooled him in gusts, when he noticed a woman craning to catch the title of his book. He held it up for her to see. *A Perfect Spy.*

A lawyer between jobs—she'd worked for NGOs in Madagascar and Mozambique—Pilar was in Oaxaca visiting a friend, taking cooking classes, and sniffing out the nonprofits. He invited her to lunch at a tiny isthmus restaurant, where they ate garnachas and he set his sights. She made it easy, correctly assuming his intent and allowing for his awkwardness. She soon followed him to Oceanside and found work with the Border Angels, but before he'd left Mexico, he took her to meet his parents. Yvette greeted her on sight with a sharp *oh!* and Claude chuckled. Until that moment, JP hadn't registered how much Pilar looked like his mother.

Claude, catching him alone, had said, "I see the attraction. Like father, like son."

Now, with his own identity in flux, he wondered about Pilar. She could be like his mother in more ways than looks. She, too, might house life-altering secrets. How would he ever know?

When Pilar slid across the sheets to kiss him good night, he turned away.

"Hey." She hooked her chin over his shoulder. "What's going on?"

"Nothing. I'm just all messed up."

"Of course you are," she said. "It's a big deal what you're going through." She gave his hip bone a little shake. "But so you know, we're at prime time."

Their code for her peak fertility.

A twinge, because he shouldn't pass this up. In fact, he couldn't bear to—at least JP Durand couldn't. But the new JP, JP Son of *Phil*, was less certain. Who were they, anyway, the two of them? Shouldn't they have a better sense of themselves—of each other—before taking this step? But could you ever know anyone? His mother had deceived him for almost thirty-four years. If he hadn't spit in that test tube, he never might have found out . . .

"You here, mi amor?" Another gentle jostling.

"Sorry," he said. "It's just my mind's going a hundred miles an hour."

"Then allow me to distract you." She clambered on top of him, tangling her legs with his.

His mind whirred on, but he did not resist.

Dear Phil Samuelson,

I recently discovered through an ancestry test that the man I knew as my father, Claude Durand, was not related to me. The test results also revealed that I have two half sisters and a half niece, who happen to be your daughters Sally, Katherine, and (I assume?) your granddaughter Eva. It would seem—and I find this as strange to write as it might be for you to read—that you are my biological father.

Yvette Joubert-Durand is my mother.

Claude passed away two years ago. He had no idea I was not his son.

If this is as big a shock to you as it was to me, I sympathize, and I'm sorry to be the bearer of such jolting news.

FYI I teach math at UCSD and am married to Pilar Ardolina. We are in Oceanside, so not far away. If you are amenable, I'd like to come up to Pasadena and meet you.

If you prefer not to be in contact, I will respect that.

Yours,
JP Durand

And in the morning, a reply:

Dear JP,

This news has come as a complete and utter surprise.

I had no idea.

Of course I want to meet you, JP. You and Pilar. ASAP!

I'd love it if you came here although I'd be equally happy to come to you or meet somewhere in between. Is next week too soon? If you came here, would you want to meet your sisters as well—or would that be too much? Happy to take it one step at a time.

Yours truly,
Phil

A few more emails and it was arranged that JP would drive to Pasadena on Friday afternoon to take a walk with Phil.

He would meet the sisters another time.

The comment lines for *Meeting birth/bio/biological father* were less angry and jaunty in tone, and more sober and realistic, with whiffs of disappointment.

Met bio dad for the first time. Truck driver, car parts counterman. I see why mom didn't hitch her wagon to his not-so-shiny star. Conversation was stop-and-go. Hard to catch up on 39 years.

> I met my new-to-me half siblings at a get-together they organized. Brought my wife. We sat around talking and eating. They remembered things about my bio dad (who died five years ago): his favorite beer (Coors), his favorite team (Patriots), his favorite snack (buffalo wings). Not the kind of people we usually socialize with. We'll no doubt see them again—they're already planning the next reunion.

"And François?" Pilar asked softly. "Have you talked to him?"

"Not yet." His older brother had inherited Claude's physical stature, nose, and occupation, so how embarrassing, how diminishing—once and for all—to concede Claude entirely to him. Anyway, François and Elise were in China for the year, on an architect's exchange program. "I'll write him, when I'm ready."

> Meeting bio dad in a few days. Curiosity and dread in equal measure.

Phil had painters at his house, he said, so he'd asked JP to meet him at his office.

In a small commercial zone that was half-shuttered but possibly on the upswing, Samuelson and Pike Engineering was sandwiched between a private law office and a party supply store festooned with piñatas. Phil Samuelson met him at the door.

His frank, open seventy-seven-year-old face showed warmth and humor. He looked JP in the eye and shook his hand. "Come in, come in."

They were the same height. Five foot nine.

JP looked away, swept by an urge to cry.

"Let me lock up the back, and we can go."

The office was clean and spare, with high ceilings, wood beams, and calm gray walls. Small. He couldn't help but think of his father's multistoried, humming architectural offices in tall downtown buildings. Here, three desks, each with large computer displays, ran along one wall. Paper maquettes of complicated buildings, museums or campuses, took up a long wooden table—appealing enough for a tiny strip mall rental.

They drove in Phil's Volvo about a mile to a trailhead on the lip of an arroyo. A narrow trail took them down to a crumbling paved road that entered the mouth of the canyon. Here, they could walk side by side. "I was so sorry to hear about Claude," said Phil.

"Thanks. Though now I don't know how to think about him. Or anything else."

"It's been a roller coaster, I'm sure. But nothing changes the fact that Claude was your father. Nothing can ever take that away."

"Though now it feels like I had no right to him." As soon as he spoke, JP heard and regretted his petulance. He sounded babyish.

A stream flowed through the trees below them. Yucca and tufts of gray-green sage grew in the cracks of the steep granite hillside.

"I'm happy to answer any questions," said Phil. "Is there anything you'd like to know?"

"All I've heard is what Yvette said, which is that Claude left the two of you alone a lot and you drank too much."

"Is that what she said?" Phil spoke quietly.

"Why, what would you say?"

"I would say we had one of those intense, close connections that happen when you're very far from home and you run into someone like-minded and sympathetic. Dhahran Aramco was a very strange place, a tiny scrap of manic Americana in the Arabian desert filled with rig drillers from Elk City, Oklahoma. Then here's your mother, so cultured and graceful and intelligent. She *shone* among those roughnecks."

"Okay!" JP said brightly, in a way that meant *Stop!* Enough with his mother's love life.

Now, in a narrow, shady stretch of canyon, the stream was more boisterous. Its gush filled the silence.

He was used to Claude and his larger-than-life, shambolic personality, his beautiful bespoke shirts untucked, his hair flying in wild white wings. His undisputed importance in any room. His comet trail of minions. What to make of this trim, soft-spoken, doe-eyed older man in a blue oxford cloth button-down, khakis, sneakers?

When a small tributary intersected their path, Phil crossed it nimbly on rocks. JP managed not to get his feet wet. Catching up to Phil, he tried on a thought—*This is my father!*—to see if it meant anything. Not really. They were the same height and shape and had a similar stride. Phil, like JP, didn't mind silence for minutes at a time.

JP watched his own feet, his black Adidas puffing up dust.

"I understand why Yvette never told me," said Phil. "Though I wish she had. Thirty-four years is a long time not to know a son."

Again, emotion swept through JP. He looked away as if to search the canyon wall for wildlife, to hide a quivering lip.

A breeze zigzagged through the treetops; clouds passed over the sun. "I love March for how changeable it is," Phil said. "Warm and sunny one minute, gloomy and freezing the next."

They talked then about the weather: the summer heat to come, Oceanside's cool sea air, Altadena's spring fogs. Pausing in an oak glen, Phil showed JP photos of his house, the freshly painted exterior: a one-story modernist post-and-beam with white rocks on the roof. JP showed photos of his condo and Pilar.

Phil peered closely. "I probably shouldn't say this but—"

"I know. I know. Everyone says so. I'm hopelessly Oedipal."

Phil laughed and it was startling, like hearing himself. Not pleasant.

They walked on, talking more easily. Phil was semiretired. And old! Though he looked good for his age. Energetic. He still ran his office, but his associates did all the drafting and fieldwork. Widowed for more than twenty years, he'd never remarried; his last girlfriend had followed her grandchildren back east. "I have my two granddaughters who pinion me here. I get them two afternoons a week."

They passed a ranger station, with its cabins and tethered barking dogs, and not long after this, Phil said, "You know my youngest, Eva, was adopted. When she was eleven, she met her birth mom, who was married with two little boys and living in Walnut Creek. A big, excited flurry followed; many phone calls back and forth. Julia—the birth mom—came to visit. Eva was bursting with their similarities: She and Julia had the same-shaped big toe! The same favorite candy bar! They both loved dogs!

"When Julia invited Eva to spend the summer at Walnut Creek, Eva was elated—but she didn't last two weeks. She'd found herself in a house full of strangers—two rambunctious little boys, a put-upon nanny, parents who worked all day. Two big sloppy dogs who did nothing but sleep. She demanded to come home."

JP understood—or thought he understood—what Phil was driving at: that they were, in fact, strangers, and that he, JP, was off the hook and preemptively excused from merging with this newfound family.

"Then, Julia invited us all to Thanksgiving, and we've had holidays together since, and many visits. It took time," Phil said, "but we're close now. Julia's son Christopher just lived with Sally's family while getting his MFA at ArtCenter."

So he was *not* off the hook! Far from it! JP pictured a line of invitations extending to infinity, each one to be politely batted away.

This was what he'd feared: a glomming on. An unsought attachment that couldn't be shaken.

They came to where the stream ran full and wide across the trail. Two older women hikers were taking off their boots and socks to cross. Phil said, "Here's where we turn around. Unless . . ."

"I'm good," said JP, so they started back. JP couldn't think what to say next. He didn't dislike the man. Or like him. And why should he feel anything for this person? When the trail widened so they could walk side by side again, Phil waited for him to catch up and said, "Would it help to know that your mother was my one and only affair?"

JP burst out, "I don't know what would help!"

Unaccountably, then, they laughed their identical laughs.

Alone and driving, he tried to make sense of his afternoon.

> Met bio dad and I found it hard to think and talk
> because I kept wondering what it meant, what I was
> supposed to feel. Mostly I felt nothing. Twice,
> I almost cried.

> At 34 yo met bio dad for the first time. He was warm and respectful and could not have been kinder.
> It was A LOT.

Once on the 57 freeway headed south, he called Pilar. "Nothing awful about him. Nice, thoughtful guy. So why do I feel like I've been beaten all over with a rubber bat?"

"It's so emotional. So huge. What you've been through."

Traffic down the 57 was annoyingly clotted in the dusk.

"He wanted us to have dinner, but I couldn't. I liked him but . . . I needed to get away."

"Any plans to see each other again?"

"He left it up to me. Whenever I'm ready."

In bed that night, he was too wound up to sleep. "Do I have to meet the sisters?"

"Don't you want to?"

"Not right now."

In moments alone—running around the track between classes, on the exercise bike at home, in bed with Pilar asleep beside him—JP ached for Claude, and felt grateful, humbled, *lucky* that Claude had raised him. It was true that Claude had never known what to make of JP's math mind (starting with his obsessive love of counting as a four-year-old), his introversion, his puniness. Claude had never called him a mama's boy, though he'd often said, "You are your mother's son." The jousting, verbal and physical, between François and Claude that invigorated them both was never extended to JP, who, all knew, would not take well to their cheerful insults, headlocks, and boxing feints.

But Claude's heavy arm had never stopped strapping him in close. Anywhere, at any time, he slung that arm across JP's shoulders ("God, Dad, not here, Dad!"); with his whiskered cheek against JP's, he'd make an observation or a joke, or say, "Your mother went to a lot of trouble with dinner, so tell her you liked it." Once, when Claude came to visit at Stanford, JP heard his raspy, uproarious voice from far down the dorm's hall and simultaneously wanted to hide and run to his embrace.

Claude, Yvette, François, and JP: that was his family, and a tight, closed system it was. Moving from Boston to Bangkok, then Jakarta, Madrid, and Oaxaca, they were a tiny country of themselves, with their own manners and customs. Every house, stone or stucco or thatched and on stilts, Yvette made familiar with her good eye and the contents (furniture, rugs, piano, and art) of a shipping container that followed them everywhere. JP had felt most himself in a family—that family—most secure and happy and known, and that's what he and Pilar had set out to create for themselves.

So. What to do with Phil? Possibly nothing. Except JP kept thinking of him. His trim, vigorous person. His balance and quickness crossing the stream on rocks. His quietness and his laugh, a softer rat-a-tat-tat. His hip, tidy, *tiny* office.

Hard to imagine Phil ever with Yvette—Yvette, who had

never been afraid of Claude, who'd stood up to him, challenged him, who'd never backed down no matter how loud he roared. Magnificent, fearless Yvette with modest, quiet, inconsequential Phil?

But here he was. Living proof.

He and Phil did have very similar hands. Same square fingers. Not that it meant anything.

> Met bio dad. Nice guy. Don't know how much I'll see him.

No invitations arrived, so none were batted away.

"Whenever you like," Phil had said, "I'm here."

JP was surprised, then, when an interest, something akin to longing, took hold.

> Met bio dad. Imagine I'll get to know him better.

"I hear you met Phil."

"How'd you hear that?"

"I had a twenty-year-old phone number that still worked. I thought I'd give him a heads-up, tell him what was barreling his way, but you got to him first. Good for you. I hear you two had a very nice hike."

JP didn't know what to say.

"We're all reeling, sweetie," said Yvette. "You, me, and Phil. He assumed that I knew all along. But really, truly I didn't. I finally had to get in the weeds with him, too."

"You didn't mention the yogurt business."

"The what? Oh, yes. I did." She laughed.

How could she laugh? But when he related this conversation to Pilar, Pilar laughed too.

Sally Samuelson lived in a big old Craftsman in west Altadena. A tall, rough-coated blond dog nosed JP at the door. "Off, Planty Pal," said a red-bearded Brit. "Terribly sorry," he said. "He has no manners. I'm Todd, Sally's husband."

Sally was right there too, in a long gray skirt, a pink pashmina knotted at her neck and disappearing under a long linen apron, her hair in a loose chignon. Gold hoop earrings. Prettier than her photos. She had sent the invitation. "So glad you're here," she said, and hugged him, then Pilar. He smelled cooking on her. Onions and spices. She gathered her two daughters. "Here's Sibbie, she's seven, and this is Ida, who's five. Girls, JP's your uncle! And here's your Aunt Pilar."

JP had a pang then for little Kai, François and Elise's three-year-old, now relegated to the same status as these shy, puny strangers. Half nieces, all.

Eva came up in a long sweater and skinny jeans and shook their hands. "So exciting," she said. "Finally, people my own age in the family."

Katie, the psychiatrist, had wanted to be there, Sally said, but she was at a conference up north.

They had not invited Phil.

"Oh, too bad," said Pilar. "I was hoping to meet him."

JP, too, had a plummet. He'd accepted Sally's invitation, he now realized, because he assumed that Phil would be here.

"Next time!" said Sally. "We wanted to get to know you on our own."

The house was full of art and books and dogs. As they moved into the living room, Planty Pal claimed a leather club chair. Eva had brought her two Italian greyhounds, who chased each other over the furniture and sprang in heart-stopping arcs off the sofa backs.

Eva taught in Claremont, but she lived here in Altadena, with her partner, Jamal, just three blocks from Sally. "Jamal wasn't invited either," Eva said. "We didn't want to deluge you with too many of us at once."

Eva was the adopted one, but also, JP was beginning to grasp, related by blood to Phil and Sally—and to him. Another niece? So confusing!

"JP, do you realize that you and I are only two months apart in age?" Eva said. "We're the in-between generation."

Was he her uncle or half brother? Pilar, who understood such things, would have to spell it out for him later.

"And did you know, JP," said Sally, "Ellis, Eva's birth dad—he'd be your half brother—was also a math whiz."

JP had never been called a math whiz. A math person. A math mind. A mathematician. Never a whiz. At least not to his face.

He was glad he'd brought Pilar because, like these women, she could talk. She told them about her work with the Border

Angels and his teaching load, and asked the questions he didn't think to ask: where did Katie fit in (she was his oldest half sister, divorced, no kids); had Phil ever mentioned Yvette (never, until "this all came out on 23andMe"); what kind of dog was Planty Pal (a lurcher, fetched as a puppy from an Irish shelter); and what did Sally and Todd do (she made art and taught it at a private primary school; Todd taught painting at ArtCenter).

The two little girls were coloring in a window seat at the far end of the room.

"Can you tell us about Yvette?" Eva said.

JP looked to Pilar for help.

"Yvette? She's very stylish and classy, very French," Pilar said. "She's in Oaxaca, and still working. She can be a little formidable, but also very funny and caring. I admire her a lot."

Sally and Eva exchanged a bright look that put JP on edge. What did they care about his mother?

Todd, pouring JP wine, leaned in. "If they get to be too much, give a signal and I'll take you out back to see the chickens."

JP drank his wine, a delicious pinot, and let the women talk. Yvette would like this house, he decided: she appreciated Craftsman architecture as a precursor to modernism. She'd want to thin it out, banish the piles. (Claude used to complain that she threw out mail and magazines before he'd had a chance to read them.) She'd set all the books upright on the shelves, replace the mismatched furniture with period-appropriate pieces, make the rooms sparer . . . cleaner . . . emptier. Of course, they'd lived sparely because they moved so much; here, life had accumulated in layers.

"We figured out when Phil knew your mom," said Sally. "It was his last trip to Saudi, a few months before our brother died. That's what's so mind-blowing: Who knew when we lost Ellis, there were already two new kids in the works? Eva and you."

JP struggled to make sense of it. A half brother who died—and now two (or was it three?) half sisters, not to mention a half niece?

Too many halves! His whole family had been halved. Halved and multiplied.

The women talked. He studied three hangings on the opposite wall, large square grids made from dyed twine, with bits of paper and cloth and words woven in: *Hollow Daydream Boulder.*

They moved into a wood-paneled dining room with a long oak table. As he sat, one of the little greyhounds leapt onto his lap.

"Just push her off," said Eva.

But he liked her there, perfectly round and shivery. She fit under the table as he slid in.

On the opposite wall hung maybe a dozen small paintings, all of clouds, by various artists; wisps to thunderheads, some white, some gray; one fat cumulus glowed as if lit from within.

Maybe he and Pilar could collect something like that—paintings of trees, perhaps. Or night skies.

The sisters had made chicken biryani with raita and a red lentil dal, some fresh chard sautéed with garlic, and soft, homemade naan. A green salad. Sibbie had crayoned name cards; his was decorated with numbers, pluses, and minuses, Pilar's had wings ("For your Border Angels," Sibbie said).

Eva was next to him; she asked in some detail about his work in design theory (which was a far cry from Pilar's brothers, who, on hearing what he did, joked that combinatorics sounded like a kitchen gadget). JP then asked Eva to describe her work with body tissues. Turned out they'd both gone to Berkeley—JP as a graduate student, Eva as a postdoc—and knew some of the same professors and even a few fellow students. Small world. It was almost weird that they'd never met.

Everyone got up to stretch their legs and clear the table for dessert.

After the blueberry cobbler, he'd had enough and appealed with a look to Pilar, who understood. "This has really been lovely," she said. "But it's a school night . . ."

"Yes, and you have miles to go," said Sally. "We're just so glad you came."

Pilar drove the hundred miles home. "What smart, interesting people," she said. "And god, what good cooks. Those two little girls are adorable. And Sally's husband—the Englishman? Todd? Did you notice how all his teeth are the exact same length, like they were filed flat that way? But what a sweetheart. I liked them all."

"I liked the chickens," said JP. While the women were clearing the table for dessert, Todd led him to the far end of a deep backyard to the run. Opening the back of the coop, he'd shone a flashlight on nine plump hens huddled together on two perches. Red, blond, white, and speckled, they shifted under the beam and chuckled softly.

"Anyway, JP." Pilar touched his knee. "You lucked out with them. They could've been anybody. But you won the lottery."

He had not entered any lottery. He'd been happy with Claude. He preferred Claude. Not this abundance.

> Met new-to-me half siblings last night: easy, smart, lively people. Good food. Many dogs and chickens. Much laughter. Completely exhausting. I'll see them again—in two years, maybe ten.

Within days, he recalled the visit more calmly, with interest, even as pleasing: the good wine, the shivery greyhound, Sibbie's name cards. The cloud paintings. Talking shop with Eva. The biryani. He had sisters.

So it wasn't two years. Or even two months. In an email, Sally invited them to a Passover seder in April. JP checked with Pilar and wrote back.

What can we bring?

Mrs. Wright

Fitz came to Sally though an old family friend, Mrs. Wright, who had been her mother's principal at Whitman Elementary. A regal, beige-haired DAR in her early fifties, Mrs. Wright had accepted an invitation to dinner at their house and despite the Samuelsons' modest, kid-disheveled home, this stern, patrician giantess had attached herself to the family. She'd come to dinner whenever Sib invited her, and if an invitation was too slow in coming, she invited herself. In turn, Mrs. Wright issued a standing invitation to tea at her home on Saturday afternoons, and Sib was hounded if she didn't attend often enough. Sally now saw that Mrs. W. was lonely—or rather, she was disciplined in managing her loneliness.

Six foot one, with formal diction, Mrs. Wright had been one of the terrors of Sally's childhood. With her hair waved like Eleanor Roosevelt's, she dominated their family dinner table, talking about her work at Camp Pendleton, where, to hear her tell it, she housed and resettled all fifty thousand Vietnamese refugees after the fall of Saigon. The family heard about the platform tents—set up in three days by the soldiers stationed at the camp—and the cold nights, the lack of warm clothes and blankets. "We served them eggs, thinking who doesn't like eggs? They didn't—that's who." Some of the refugees volunteered to cook, and "made their own exquisite cuisine, and everyone began to eat. You know, they taught the French a thing or two about food." Mrs. Wright had also coordinated a small army of volunteers to teach English to the adults and children. "We started the children on nursery rhymes; in weeks, they were chattering in English. The adults of course took longer."

They heard too about her first husband, the brilliant astrophysicist Robert Wright, who died young; and her second husband, Tom Kellogg (yes, of cereal family fame), who turned out to be a hopeless alcoholic—she left him after less than a year and took back her first husband's name. She doted on Phil. "He's a very handsome man," declared Mrs. Wright, and Sib was "a very lucky woman." To Sally, these pronouncements came down from on high.

She and her baby sister, Eva, were often dragged to Saturday tea. Mrs. Wright's Cliff May ranch-style home sat on a wooded half acre in a hushed, wealthy Pasadena neighborhood. They rarely encountered any other guests, although a few times they arrived as a small group of Asians—former refugees—were leaving.

Mrs. Wright made real tea with leaves in a pot and served it in fine flowered china cups with thin, chocolate-coated wafers.

Sally and Eva gamboled with the dachshund, Hansi, on the vast back lawn or in the carpeted living room, where Sally wrapped Hansi in a pink mohair throw as if he were a baby. Meanwhile Mrs. Wright talked about her refugees—*They had small bags of belongings, all that was left of their lives*—and tutored Sib in educational theory and school district politics. (Sib became a fearless, pioneering educator in the Pasadena school system.) At some point, Mrs. Wright would call out to Sally and demand to know her interests, the books she liked, the musical instrument she played. Did she have friends? Sally should bring them along to visit her. She adored young people.

She adores scaring young people, Sally told her mother.

Sally was almost twenty and in college when Sib died of breast cancer. Mrs. Wright spoke movingly at the memorial service about Sib's great abilities as a teacher. "Sibyl Samuelson was as clever and energetic a woman as I ever met," she said. "And she married a handsome, lovely man."

She and Phil kept in touch, and she came to Sally's wedding ten years later, giving her a beautiful large oval copper roasting pan that Sally often uses, along with the pink handwoven mohair throw in which she had once enfolded Hansi.

For the next eight years, Sally was lost in marriage and babies, and trying to make art while also running a small custom blinds and curtains business. She didn't give much thought to Mrs. Wright until she and Todd ran into her at the opera, where she was flanked by two beautifully dressed gay men in their forties. In her late seventies, still tall and impeccable in a sage-colored suit, her bottle-beige hair still precision waved à la Eleanor, Mrs. Wright wasted no time in issuing commands.

"You must come to tea this Saturday," she said. "Bring your children. I haven't even met them."

Sally took Sibbie and Ida. The garden was still perfectly kept, the house a little worn at the edges but spotless and bright. The two little girls loved Max, Hansi's second replacement (Sally had missed a Willi entirely), and were as intimidated by his owner as Sally had been. But they, too, loved the capacious china cups, the thin cookies, the tolerant dachshund, and the stories about a clever grandmother they'd never met.

Mrs. W. was still living alone and driving, but not at night. She was writing a memoir about the refugees and was as vigilant against loneliness as ever. "The Boys"—the gay couple Sally met at the opera—took her to plays and concerts and cooked Sunday supper for her. "The Gals"—her housekeepers—came twice a week. And in between there was her handyman/gardener/arborist, Fitz.

Fitz—Fitznorman Brown—worked for Mrs. Wright two days a week; he did whatever the mow-and-blow guys didn't: he pruned her trees and shaped the ancient, woody camellias, built trellises and planter boxes, hand-watered, dug flower beds, tended a small vegetable plot. He carried the tea tray outside and back. Mrs. Wright, a liberal Democrat, once instructed Fitz, in Sally's hearing, to make the yard "look Republican."

"Fitz is a treasure," Mrs. Wright said. "He is extremely good-natured and easygoing. Too easygoing."

Fitz worked hard, she went on—he was in and out of earshot of her; she never cared—but he needed to work *more.* He was not a go-getter. To build up his client base, she was asking all her friends to hire him. He had a family to feed—two daughters and a new baby here in Pasadena, three other children with an ex-wife in Jamaica. "You must take him one day a month, if not two," she said. "He is not expensive and he will transform your garden."

Sally and Todd did need help with their large, messy yard, so Fitz became a mainstay in their lives, coming two or three times a month to rake up the eucalyptus leaves, deadhead the roses, sweep the decks, weed. In Jamaica, he had been a cook in the military and a schoolteacher in civilian life; here, as he took the slow path to citizenship, he worked as a handyman/gardener for maybe a dozen people. He was intelligent, worldly, culturally attuned; he and Sally watched the same television shows and shared the same politics. She often gardened side by side with him; they had long conversations about their lives, and they gossiped shamelessly about Mrs. Wright—the Boys, the Gals, the dachshund.

When Sally and Todd first hired Fitz, he and his wife, Alma, had three children; over the next seven years, they had three more. Sally passed on her girls' hand-me-downs, and bought his girls new dresses for confirmations, proms, and graduations. Mrs. Wright sent the two oldest to a good Catholic school, as the public school in their neighborhood was "not what it used to be." The middle kids went to a charter school, also thanks to Mrs. W.'s intervention. Alma made food for Mrs. Wright during the week, and Sally hired Alma to help her out at parties. When deluged with blind and curtain orders, Sally asked Alma to sew with her. They all came to rely on one another and, allowing for all the usual employer-employee constraints—Fitz, with some hilarity, called Sally Boss Lady and Mrs. Wright Madame and Madame Boss Lady—their lives intertwined, and they became close, and very like friends.

Fitz had been working for Sally and Todd for six years when his mother came to visit from Jamaica. He brought her by to meet them.

Linda Brown was a small sturdy woman in her midseventies dressed in the T-shirt, jeans, and sneakers of a teenager. Like Fitz, she loved to laugh. As Sally made tea (using tea bags and coffee mugs), Fitz told a story about how he had just bought a seven-year-old Lincoln Navigator at a car auction and had driven it less than a mile when it began to make a terrible grinding noise. *Grrrttt, grrrttt.*

Sally felt bad for Fitz and his rotten luck: he needed a large car for his family, but why one so expensive to maintain, and why buy it at an auction when he couldn't even test-drive it? She expected maternal disapproval, but Linda slapped her knees and laughed cheerfully at this doleful tale, especially when Fitz went *Grrrttt, grrrttt.*

Linda took her mug of PG Tips with four teaspoons of sugar. Sally understood none of the patois she used with Fitz, but she spoke clear, lilting English to her, and was lively and warm. Linda's husband, long dead, had been a lawyer—"A lawyer to the poor so we stayed poor too," Fitz added. Linda had worked in her husband's law office until she had four children, then quit to tend them and six more. All ten were living.

Between her six kids in Jamaica and the four in California, she had twenty-seven grandchildren and four great-grandchildren. She alone knew all the names and ages. On this visit, she was meeting the California grandkids for the first time.

She refused a second cup of tea because they were on their way to Mrs. Wright's.

Linda stayed for months, floating from one son to the next, babysitting and cooking and giving each family much-appreciated support in turn. Fitz was always happy when she landed at his house—"It is the only time I can take Alma out for a hamburger," he said. One Saturday, Sally found not only Fitz working at Mrs. Wright's but also Linda, who was setting out the cups, milk, and sugar for tea in the yard. It was a cool autumnal afternoon and Mrs. Wright was in her chair under the tree, a green mohair throw over her legs.

"Linda wanted some pocket money so she comes here twice a week with Fitz, but frankly, I'd like to get her full-time," said Mrs. Wright. "She says I don't work her half as hard as her grandkids do."

So far as Sally could tell, Linda's tasks were making tea, preparing a little lunch, and binge-watching old movies with Mrs. Wright. Linda had learned from her teenage grandkids how to operate the cable and the Apple TV.

"She's very intelligent," Mrs. Wright said in front of Linda. "And technologically up-to-date. I call her my remote controller. That's what happens when you have teenagers in your life. You have someone on hand who knows how to operate a television. It's the one regret I have, never having children."

"I give you half of mine," said Linda.

The way Mrs. Wright always said that Sally's father was handsome and her mother clever, she said of Fitz and Linda that they were good-natured. "The whole family has a marvelous temperament," Mrs. Wright said. "When I'm alone at night, I think, *Tomorrow or the next day, Linda will come and I will hear her laugh.*"

"Those two," Fitz told Sally. "They laugh and cackle together like witches."

Linda soon took a bus to Mrs. Wright's house four afternoons a week.

"She really knows her way around a computer. She pays my

bills, and makes my charitable contributions online, and she's typed up some of my memoir. She has made some excellent editorial suggestions."

One Saturday, Linda answered the door and led Sally to the living room. "Don't sit too close," Linda instructed. "Today she bites!"

"Bad news from my tax man," said Mrs. Wright.

"He quit!" Linda said and slapped her leg. "Moved to Mexico!"

"It's not funny!" said Mrs. Wright.

"I call it good news!" Linda said. "For twenty years, he charged her a thousand! A thousand, for a couple little forms! And her income not so complicated: pension, investments, charitable contributions. Two hours with TurboTax and I have it done. And no charge to Madame!" She put her hand on Mrs. Wright's shoulder and gave it a little shake. "All my sons, I do their taxes, no audits! Even Tobias's construction business—now that's complicated. But same price! A cup of tea. And a 'Thank you very much, beautiful Linda.'"

"A cup of tea!" said Mrs. Wright. "Let's have one, beautiful Linda."

Linda went to put on the kettle.

Mrs. Wright watched her go. "She is beautiful, beautiful, my Linda."

Mrs. Wright bought Linda an iPhone and a used Subaru so she didn't have to take the bus and could run errands. Mrs. Wright paid for the car insurance and gave her a credit card to buy gas and household goods. When her family could spare her, Linda slept over in the pretty guest bedroom.

"She speaks and writes the Queen's English when she wants to," said Mrs. Wright. "She is quite perceptive, and her suggestions for the memoir are brilliant—she understands the immigrant far better than I do. She also does research for me on the internet. We have become close collaborators; I've decided to give her coauthorship. I don't know what I would do without her."

One hot September afternoon Sally found Fitz and Linda and Alma in the shady backyard drinking tea with Mrs. Wright and laughing.

"Tell her, Mama, what you just told us," Fitz said, but before Linda could answer, he added, "She wants to get married! She is looking for Mr. Right."

"Do you know someone who might want an old lady, not too fat?" said Linda.

"Aren't you busy enough already?" said Sally.

"That's exactly what I said," said Alma. "Why take on a husband?"

"Her visa expired months ago," Mrs. Wright cut in. "If she goes back to Jamaica, she can't get another visa for ten years. But if she marries an American citizen, she can get a green card and start the path to citizenship."

"That is what I did," said Fitz. "I married Alma and after a very, very, very long time, I got my green card."

Two of his other brothers here in California also married Americans and were limping toward citizenship. Only Algernon—the one nicknamed Gauntlet—hadn't married the mother of his four Californian children, but that was because he still had a wife in Jamaica.

"Gauntlet's visa expired seven years ago," said Fitz. "It is no problem if you avoid ICE and don't leave the country."

There were three new great-grandchildren in Jamaica Linda wanted to meet. But she also wanted to return to California. "If I got me a little old fellow with a place, I could come and go."

"Good luck," Alma said. "I don't know if you've noticed, Linda, but men your age are mostly dead. And if they're not, they're looking for a nurse with a purse."

"Oh, there must be some old widow man who likes hot soup."

"I suppose there's Refugio," said Mrs. Wright, offering her sprinkler-and-gutter man. "You two already have a little spark. Don't deny it."

"Ah, Refugio," Linda said. "We laugh. But he lives with a lady. And anyway, I would not take a Spanish. People should stay with their own."

"How can you say that with Alma here—lovely Alma, who has your grandbabies, and is such a good wife to your rascal son?" Mrs. Wright had drawn up to her most imperious.

"I love Alma," said Linda. "But to marry, I want an island man. Smart and easy and just enough rich."

"If you're serious about keeping a toehold in California," Mrs. Wright said, "you might have to widen your net."

"Maybe I'm serious. I have not been married since my husband died," Linda said. "Twenty-one years now. Him I knew since we were two years old. Oh, what a great big laughing man with big smart forehead—my son Gauntlet, he has that forehead. A windshield for his big brain. And all my children laugh like him."

"Oh, lord," said Fitz. "He was an evil demon. He would line us up to go anywhere, his own army. On the bus, he would not let the driver move until he called all our names, the terrible names he gave us: "Fitznorman, Penelope, Samson, Hector, MacHenry, Larissa, Robertson, Isolde, Tobias, Algernon. We were so embarrassed. *Stop it, Daddy; be quiet Daddy.* We hated it!"

"And when he drank the rum!" Linda slapped her knee. "He rampage through the town. He set one foot on Talus Road, and people hollered up the street so the children could go to their hidey-holes before the chairs and tables start to fly." She and Fitz laughed; Alma and Sally shared strained smiles. Mrs. Wright sat stiff and upright, beaming disapproval.

Days later, at her own house, Sally asked Fitz, "How can you laugh about your father's drunken rampages?"

"When you can laugh, that means it is over."

Fitz was raking in Sally's backyard on a chilly November day. She went out to see him. "How you doing, Boss Lady?" he said. "Have you heard the news?"

He was bursting to say it. "Madame says that *she* will marry my mother."

Sally was struck silent for a moment. "Wow," she said. "That's pretty brilliant."

"She says now, women can marry women. And they have been so close for two years, they could pass all the INS interviews. Linda's name is on checks and a credit card; she knows all of Madame's habits. And Madame knows the names of all the grandchildren. Madame even says that she loves her! She loves Linda."

Both Sally and Fitz burst out laughing.

"But wouldn't they have to live together?"

"Madame wants that," said Fitz. "And Linda already gets her mail there."

"And your mother—Linda—has she said yes?"

"She doesn't answer. To me, she says, 'It is not right. Even if Madame was a man, there is too much difference.' But to Madame . . . she says nothing. She is afraid to hurt her feelings. Or make her mad. But mostly, Linda laughs and laughs."

On Saturday afternoon, Sally found Linda and Mrs. Wright hunched on low green plastic stools on the grass, dividing and bagging iris bulbs that Fitz was digging up. Nobody was laughing.

Mrs. Wright, elbows on knees, hands covered in dirt, looked up at Sally. "Have you heard that I have asked Linda to marry me?"

"I heard that you asked, but not the answer." Sally looked brightly at Linda.

Linda placed some muddy rhizomes in a plastic bag and discomfort, like a shadow, passed over her face. "I cannot answer that."

Mrs. Wright said, "You say you want to stick with your kind."

"Lord, yes."

Fitz laughed very loud at this. "Linda, Mama, you have been waiting so long for your Mr. Right. Only the mister is a missus."

"That is my point," said Linda. "She is a woman."

"Nobody's perfect," said Mrs. Wright.

"I know that movie," said Sally.

"Lord God," Linda said—with clear pain.

"Two Wrights don't make a wrong," Sally said, hoping to preserve—or reinstate—some levity.

Three people laughed. Linda looked steadily at the grass.

The Subaru was parked in Mrs. Wright's driveway, but Sally did not see Linda when she visited the house. Mrs. Wright was sad and irritable. "One of her Oceanside granddaughters had leg surgery, and Linda has gone to nurse her. Fitz took her to the train. I'm afraid my offer offended her, or she never would've left."

"She'll get over it," said Sally.

"I thought we could be happy," Mrs. Wright went on. "But Linda finds the whole idea distasteful and ungodly. As if being married to a violent drunkard was somehow more respectable."

"Marrying her was a very creative idea," Sally said. "And so generous."

"Not really," said Mrs. Wright. "I proposed because I love her. And I believe she loves me. She just can't admit it."

"Maybe she needs to get used to the idea," said Sally. "Maybe same-sex marriage is a little too progressive for her."

"I'd put her on my pension, too, which she would have for life, after I'm gone." She leaned down to pet Max's smooth tan head. "I do love her, don't I, little Maxie?" she said in a soft, sweet tone Sally had never heard before. "I do love my Linda."

Linda stayed in Oceanside throughout the fall. Fitz kept Sally up-to-date, and urged her to visit Mrs. Wright, who was very low and cranky. Sally found it disquieting to see the terror of her childhood so listless.

"Madame is getting very thin," Fitz reported. "And very old."

Indeed, by January, Mrs. Wright seemed newly fragile and unsteady on her feet as Sally followed her to the living room. "How's the memoir?" she asked.

"I have given it up," said Mrs. Wright, lifting one hand, then letting it drop.

"But you had such times with the refugees."

"Too long ago. All just a dream."

Mrs. Wright's imperiousness and certainty, her absolute sense of how the world should run—however much Sally agreed or disagreed with her—had formed a kind of bedrock in Sally's life, and seeing her so subdued, resigned, and frail was quite destabilizing. Sally enlisted her teenage daughters to cheer up the old woman, but Mrs. Wright was unresponsive, and even failed to interrogate them.

Mrs. Wright sure misses your mom."

Fitz was reshaping the wells around her roses when Sally brought him a glass of sweet tea. "Yes, she misses her remote controller. And my mother, too, is very sad," said Fitz. "They had good times, those two old witch ladies. Always very busy together. At our houses Linda cooks and straightens up and runs after the kids; Mrs. Wright's is much more interesting to her. There, she uses her brain. There she has a good friend. But the last time they talked, Madame got very angry and now Linda says she can't ever return."

"Of course she can," Sally said. "And she should just marry Mrs. Wright. It's the perfect solution to her immigration dilemma. And they do adore each other."

Fitz loosened the soil at the base of a rosebush and scraped it outward to form a shallow moat. "My mother has her old ideas. She says people will think they have 'relations.' She doesn't want the grandkids to hear that talk."

"That's ridiculous," Sally said.

"I told her, I said, 'Mama, Linda, at your age nobody will think of you having relations with anyone.'" Fitz stabbed the dirt with the point of his spade. "Especially not with Madame."

"That is a terrifying idea," Sally said. "Relations with Mrs. Wright."

On a rainy Saturday in February, Fitz's daughter Stephanie answered Mrs. Wright's door. She and Alma had brought over food. "She hardly eats," Alma whispered to Sally in the kitchen. "She sits all day doing nothing."

"And how's Linda?"

"Also not good. She can leave Oceanside anytime she wants and come to us. But she can't get it together. She says she doesn't feel well. Woman trouble. Gauntlet took her to the doctor who said she was fine, just depressed."

Sally screwed up her courage and went into the living room. Mrs. Wright was on the sofa in her ivory blouse and sturdy at-home gabardine skirt. Also: her usual nude nylons—where did she even find them these days?—and snub-toed flats. Sally sat beside her and put a hand on her upper arm—had she ever touched her before? "Mrs. Wright," she said. "Maybe it's time to bring Linda back. Tell her you won't mention marriage again."

Mrs. Wright fluffed her hair, which was thinner but still uniformly beige and precision-waved. "But I do want to marry her. I want to spend the rest of my life with her. What the two of us have is far firmer ground for a marriage than the crazy infatuation that led me to marry that Kellogg fellow. Or even Robert Wright."

A question formed, and Sally knew she had to ask it. She tried to sound casual. "But what about sex and all that?"

Mrs. Wright waved this away. "My old parts dried up long ago," she said. "I don't care about sex. But who knew, in my old age, love would come again?"

Now Sally put a hand on her wrist. "But what if marriage is too great a leap for Linda? Even if she feels as deeply about you."

Mrs. Wright set down her teacup. "A few years ago, same-sex marriage was illegal. If a whole country can change its thinking, one smart Jamaican lady can come around."

"Most of a country, at least," said Sally.

"For centuries, men and women have married each other for all sorts of accommodations," Mrs. Wright continued, with some of her old imperiousness. "Marriage is always to some degree strategic; once it was the only way a woman could better herself or secure a decent future, with or without love. Today, women can marry women for all the many reasons women have married men." She gathered herself. "I'm a good strategy for Linda. I'll put her name on the house. I was planning to leave it to her anyway. She'll get half my pension to cover the upkeep and taxes. She could downsize or move in one or more of her kids. It would set her and the family up." Mrs. Wright's posture softened and with it, her voice. "You know, Linda and I actually have love, if only she could admit it."

"Why not just ask her to come back, with everything as it was before?"

"I have gone too far for that. I could not muster the pretense required."

"Oh, Mrs. Wright," Sally said. "Maybe you could."

Perhaps Mrs. Wright would have wasted away that winter and died at eighty-seven. And Linda would have hidden out in Oceanside for months to come. But something happened that changed everything. The lumberyard where Gauntlet worked was raided, and he was swept up along with the day laborers stationed at the entrance and swiftly deported, first sent by bus to Galveston, then flown from there to Kingston.

Fitz missed several weeks of work to help the mother of Gauntlet's kids pack up and get everyone's passports, so they could join him in Jamaica before the first, legal wife reclaimed him.

When Fitz again came to Sally and Todd's house, he and Sally sat in the kitchen with mugs of tea. Sally asked if he'd gotten everything squared away. "Oh yes, very squared," he said humorously, then laughed out loud.

"Tell me," Sally said.

"Everyone left on Friday. I told Linda she could go home too, that I would buy her a ticket. She said no. So she is with us now, and terrified of being deported. She won't even go to the market."

"You can't blame her—she's traumatized."

"I told her, I said, 'Mama, Linda, don't worry: if you get sent home, your American boys will come visit. We won't forget you.' And she said, 'I don't worry about you or your brothers.' And I said, 'I know, Mama, you are worried that the grandchildren here will grow up not knowing you.' And she said, 'They already know me. I'm not worried about that.' And I said, 'It's awful to be deported, treated like cattle, fed rotten food, but they don't beat you.' And she said, 'I don't worry that they'll beat me.' So I said, 'Then what are you worried about?' And do you know what she said, Boss Lady?"

Sally ventured a guess. "She's worried about making a living in Jamaica?"

"Lord no," said Fitz. "She will always be taken care of. No. She said, 'I worry about Madame. She is too old and alone, and our book is not finished.'"

"Does this mean that she is finally coming around?"

"Lord, and what a long way around it has been. They are meeting today." Fitz checked his phone. "Almost now."

It had to be a real wedding, with printed invitations, a guest list, a meal, a minister, a cake. Sally offered to help with the invitations and brought over some samples of fonts and papers. While the two women considered their options, Sally sketched them in black ink on a piece of cardstock: Linda was pointing out a font and looking over with a smile at Mrs. Wright, who, sitting bolt upright and peering down through her reading glasses, also appeared highly amused.

"What a clever drawing," said Mrs. Wright. "It looks quite like us. I had no idea you had such skill."

"Lord, look how straight you sit," Linda said. "And me, all hunched over."

"You look sly as ever," said Mrs. Wright. "Like you are having a good laugh at yours truly."

"I always am," said Linda. "That much is true."

Somehow, Sally had captured a moment of happiness.

Fitz came over for a look. "There is your invitation," he said.

Indeed, when set above the printed portion, the drawing looked as if Linda was pointing to, and Mrs. Wright was peering down at, the following:

Mrs. Linda Brown and Mrs. Winona Wright
Request the Honor of Your Presence
at Their Marriage
on Sunday the Seventeenth of April
at Eleven in the Morning
in the Year Two Thousand Fourteen

Fifty white rental chairs were set up with an aisle down the middle in the backyard, which Fitz and the gardeners had groomed to garden-tour, Republican perfection. Nearby, seven round tables, with white cloths and centerpieces of pink peonies, were clustered in the shady spots. Most of those who employed Fitz—Sally, her sister Eva, and all the others whom Mrs. Wright had exhorted to hire him—were present, as were Fitz's two tall, rangy California brothers and their families.

Sally's two girls, and two of Fitz's, had gone shopping together for dresses with her credit card and they might have been teleported from a prom for all their backless, strapless, sequined splendor. Fitz's sons wore rented tuxes. The photographers were Todd and Fitz's oldest girl, Stephanie, now in a high school for the arts; she was gorgeous and stately in a floral-print sari and hot pink turban.

The Boys stood as witnesses—they'd signed the marriage certificate beforehand in the den. When a string trio launched into the wedding march, the Gals stepped out of the kitchen, where they'd been assisting the caterers, and took seats as Mrs. Wright and Linda walked down the grassy aisle. A few minutes late, seven elderly Vietnamese, four men and three women, quietly filed into the back rows. Max, having escaped from the house with them, wriggled joyously through the assembled, petted and scratched by all.

In the shade of a magnificent oak, the women stopped and faced each other. A young female Unitarian Universalist minister conducted the service. "It is written that the greatest of all things is love," she said. "And wherever there is love, that which is holy abides there also. . . ."

Mrs. Wright stood still and tall in her sage-green suit—she had a good eight inches on Linda. Yet it was Linda, in a royal blue pantsuit, who reached out and took her bride's hands.

Phil

On the morning of his second wedding day, Phil Samuelson finds himself thinking of his first.

He is walking to the hotel where his children are staying, down in the Centro district of Oaxaca. Yvette had a very early hair appointment in the Xochimilco neighborhood, so Phil went that far with her by car, and is going the rest of the way on foot. He promised to meet the kids for breakfast, around nine. It is not quite eight on a fine sunny Saturday morning, still chilly in the shadows. He meets only a few early marketers lugging their bulging shopping bags up the hill.

His first wedding day was also a Saturday, and—he does the math—almost fifty-five years ago.

He comes to a small park, the Conzatti, where a dog, a tall red hound, always greets him. And here he comes. Too sleek and well fed for a stray—although, in keeping with the local custom, he is not neutered—he lopes up to Phil, and together they walk the stone-paved paths. Phil can't help but feel chosen, anointed.

He was nineteen years old when a family friend subdivided the lemon grove around the corner from his childhood home. He had some money saved from working construction in the summers and on weekends during high school and community college. The friend gave him a good deal on a quarter-acre lot.

It's hard to imagine now, but back then, a hardworking kid could buy a nice piece of real estate in Altadena with a few years' savings.

His first two years as a property owner, he was an upperclassman at USC and spent what spare time he had chopping down lemon trees. Twenty out of the twenty-four on the property. He borrowed a tractor to pull out the roots.

He'd waffled between majoring in architecture or civil engineering until his surveying professor said that engineers "made the money." He had a house to build. He wanted the money.

He graduated and passed the first qualifying exam. His architecture professor offered him an internship at his firm, work experience he needed to take the second exam. He lived at home with his mother to save money and work on his property. Eventually, he had a house site graded. He dug the footings by himself.

Once the foundation was poured, he started in on the framing. He'd worked one summer on a framing crew—they could frame a three-bedroom in a day. Flying solo was a lot slower, but once the frame was up and he walked room to skeletal room, he had a powerful urge to fill the place. To populate it.

Funny the forces that shape a person's life.

He met Sib less than two weeks later at a gathering of the Socialist Club. She was visiting from Philadelphia and had come with her cousin Jerry, who wanted to make a lefty out of her. In her beige pleated skirt and silky white blouse, with her piled-up brown curls and bright red lipstick, she stood out among the motley socialists like a big blooming flower, a cream-colored rose. He asked Jerry to introduce him.

Phil Samuelson, meet Sibyl Hartstein.

Her attention drooped when she heard he lived with his mother. But how it perked up when he said he was an engineer and building a house he'd designed.

A cellist with a degree in performance from Peabody, Sib came from a wealthy Melrose Park family of Viennese Jews. She took on Phil's cultural education, inviting him to concerts and plays and art museums. He took her to socialist meetings, on architectural tours of Los Angeles, and hiking in the San Gabriels. She had never hiked before, but took to the mountains like a little goat, agile and peppy. After some months, she agreed to go camping with him. For a young single woman to go off with a man for the weekend back then was bold, but she assured her aunt that she'd keep the tent post between them. And she did.

Sib and her brothers had gone to sleepover camp in Maine as

kids, and the whole family went to massive resort hotels in the Catskills, but nobody she knew went *camping*. She loved everything about it: the nest of pots and pans, the Coleman cookstove, the army surplus canvas tent. She was amazed that you could wash dishes in a rubber tub with water heated on the stove and cook potatoes wrapped in foil in a campfire.

She was very energetic. She loved the fresh air, the scenery.

He proposed at Mineral King after a long uphill hike, at a spectacular viewpoint: they could see the whole snow-covered spine of the Sierra Nevadas. He offered up the small, all-he-could-afford diamond ring and she said, *Yes*.

Phil looks up into the black-green crowns of the Conzatti's laurel trees. Nearby, a wide, bubbling pond adds its bright notes to the city's morning thrum. The dog leans amiably against his shin.

They married six months after they met. He was twenty-three, Sib twenty-one.

She insisted on a quick, secular ceremony, with no "superstitious folderol, or stupid cake." (Religion, she liked to say, just got people into trouble.) So, no rabbi, no huppah, no smashing a glass. They set the date in early September because her parents would be in town then. (She had assured them that he was, or would soon be, "a professional.") Sib and her aunt arranged the wedding details, while his job was to make the new house habitable. He was up till one in the morning the night before the wedding painting and getting the bathroom functional. (When he finally connected the water to the sink, he'd reversed the hot and cold faucets. He never did put it to rights. To this day, when faced with taps, he stops to think which is the hot and which the cold.)

The morning of that wedding day, almost fifty-five years ago, he woke early. He washed the car, then himself; he put on his new suit, and drove to Sib's aunt's house in the Hollywood Hills, where they were married in a dim airless living room with only his mother, Sib's parents, various cousins, and two of his friends looking on. He could barely breathe. Sib's hair had been newly permed into fluff. A big, gawping orchid pinned to her jacket lolled its frilly, speckled tongue at him throughout the ceremony. The officiant was a friend of Sib's aunt, a judge who later became the state attorney general, California's first Jewish attorney general.

The lunch afterward was on the patio. Brisket and knishes, he can't remember what else. They sat at a card table. Someone filled their champagne glasses, and someone else brought them plates of food, but they were too polite to eat while people came up to congratulate them.

Despite all of Sib's interdictions, a small, tiered cake crowned with a plastic couple appeared on the buffet table. They cut into it—the photographer insisted—but Sib refused to feed Phil any or taste the chunk he held out to her. They left in a rain of rice—again, to Sib's dismay.

Someone had put a bottle of champagne and two glasses in

the car. While he drove, Sib popped the cork, handed him a glass, filled it and her own, laughing raucously every time the champagne foamed over on their good clothes. He'd never cared for champagne and had already had more than enough at the lunch, but he drank a glass or two just to keep Sib from downing too much after so many toasts and so little to eat.

Once they were on the Angeles Crest Highway she passed out and slept the rest of the way. He set up camp by himself, then wrangled Sib through her ablutions and into her sleeping bag. He built a fire and stared into it. The permanence hit him.

Not the most romantic wedding night a man ever had.

The morning after, a hungover Sib grew increasingly quiet and withdrawn. He asked what was wrong and she began to cry. She was afraid, she said, that he was poor, and *lower class*, and that she had come down in the world by marrying him.

He had jollied her into a better mood, calling her "a bad socialist" and "a big bag of regrets." He soon had her laughing and marveling at the nearby granite crags and then discussing what they should have for dinner, sloppy joes or beef stew.

Still. Whenever he'd worn an old or stained shirt around the house, or made a noise blowing his nose, she'd said, "Your shtetl roots are showing, Phil."

She never forgot that she'd married below her station.

Nobody from his first wedding day—none of the cousins, the parents, the judge, or either of his friends—is still alive. He saw the judge's obit eight or nine years ago. After he was the state attorney general, he became the longest-serving member of the state supreme court. Who knew?

Sib herself has been gone for twenty-four years now.

Even the groom, young Phil Samuelson, has ceased to exist. He's been replaced by this capitalist alter kaker sitting in the sun in the Jardín Conzatti in Oaxaca, Mexico, who later today will marry the only other woman he slept with in his thirty-odd-year marriage.

He stretches and stands. The dog accompanies him to the southeast corner of the little park and watches from the curb as Phil walks away.

He moves on to the Llano, a larger, rectangular, sunny park usually full of families and exercise classes, though it's quiet at this time of the morning. This is where JP first met Pilar, and Phil claims the very bench near the fountain where their swift courtship and now-growing family began.

His own years as a young family man are a pleasant haze. Things weren't perfect—Ellis came earlier than they might have wanted, a month before their first anniversary, when Phil was still nailing baseboards and plastering drywall in the baby's room. Once they saw that crinkled red face, though, they were ambushed by happiness. Two years later, a miscarriage broke their hearts. Katie finally arrived three and a half years after Ellis.

Sib was an ardent mother; she joined a mothers' group when Ellis was a few months old and soon was the leader. They put Ellis into a cooperative nursery school and within six months she was elected the board president. She had energy to burn. Starting when both kids were only a month old, she and Phil took them on hikes and camping trips—the Kern River, Sequoia, Julian, Anza-Borrego, the Sierras, Big Sur. Soon, there were excursions to the San Diego Zoo, the Monterey Bay Aquarium. Puppet shows, movies, museums.

Two kids was what they wanted. A boy and a girl. By the time Katie was in kindergarten, Sib was done with nursery school boards, not to mention diapers, cribs, and nursing. She was set to enroll in education classes at Pasadena City College.

Then came Sally. The shock of that pregnancy never fully ebbed into gladness, but Sib was resigned to it—and she'd always loved a baby. Sally was no exception. "But then the will starts forming," Sib used to say.

She hired a babysitter three afternoons a week so she could teach cello in a room she rented at a nearby Catholic church. She had to do *something*, she said.

Phil thought things would improve when he got the job at Parsons, which doubled his previous salary. They hired Socorro to help around the house so Sib could go back to school, this time to a vaunted program at USC. She was so anxious on her first day, he had to drive her to campus and walk her to class. Her teeth were literally chattering, the poor thing.

Soon enough, school took her over.

Sally has occasionally said, "At some point, Mom turned sort of mean."

He knows. Because he felt it too: once Sib went to school and started to work, she became an independent unit, too often treating the rest of them as bothersome roommates. The first thing she did when she got home, even before she greeted anyone, was to pour some Hawaiian Punch into a green plastic tumbler and then, bending over, as if sneaking it—she never lifted the bottle higher than her knees—she'd add a hefty lash of the vodka she kept under the sink. She then carried this tumbler, which she stealthily replenished, as she ate dinner, did her homework and later her class prep, till she went to bed. They learned to tiptoe around her. To not disturb.

No wonder Ellis stayed away from home that summer after graduating. At least he had that time with his friends, his job, his love.

Phil, too, had been happy to get away when Parsons started sending him out of the country to oil installations in Argentina and, when his Arabic got good enough, to infrastructure projects in Jeddah, Saudi Arabia, and to an almost-finished airport in Dhahran. That was still the high point of his working life: going around the world to places he never dreamed he'd see.

Before his trip to Dhahran, Phil and Sib had gone to a Christmas party at the new Pasadena headquarters and met some engineers and project managers who lived over there but were home for the holidays. Ruth Matthews, the loud, rowdy wife of a petroleum engineer, teased Sib about "letting" her husband go to Saudi alone because "all sorts of wild things" went on in the Aramco compounds there. "One of those wives might pounce on him."

"On *Phil*?" Sib said. "Don't make me laugh."

When his affair came to light, thirty-five years after the fact, in the form of a thirty-four-year-old son, his daughters, fueled by wine, ganged up on him one night, volleying questions at him that none of them would have had the temerity to ask him one-on-one.

Had he been unhappy with Sib?

To some degree, he supposed.

Was there drinking involved with Yvette?

Not a significant amount. A couple of drinks.

How long did it go on?

Nine or ten days, maybe.

Was she using any birth control?

That didn't come up.

Why didn't it come up?

It just didn't.

Was he using birth control?

That was getting a little personal.

Suddenly getting a new brother is a little personal too. Had he seen Yvette since?

Once, when checking out Thacher for Eva; she was checking it out for JP. A total coincidence.

And what happened then?

They had lunch and caught up with each other.

No spark?

A hesitation. He would say there was a spark.

She had a boy around Eva's age and he didn't do the math or think for a second that JP might have been his?

She hadn't said anything, so why would he think of that?

Has he been in love with her all these years?

He had always thought fondly of her, when he thought of her. But many other things were going on.

Did Sib ever find out or suspect anything?

He always wondered.

A tai chi class has formed in the grassy space ahead. Maybe fifteen people moving in slow motion in unison.

Sometimes, it seemed Sib had known something. Or sensed it. She had been suspicious of the pearls he gave her on his return from Dhahran. "What brought this on?" she'd said, picking open the wrinkled tissue he'd wrapped them in. The large, snow-white spheres had come on nylon filament—fishing line—and when she had them restrung, the jeweler told her what they were worth. "I wish he hadn't because now I'm afraid to wear them out in public," she said. And she never had.

But they were not a guilt offering. He had bought them before he had anything to feel guilty about. Well, some hours before.

(Sally was wearing the pearls last night at the restaurant. And Yvette was wearing the yellow ones he'd bought her. This had made him unaccountably happy.)

Phil has to pull in his legs as half a dozen boys on skateboards veer close.

So much had happened right after Dhahran, it was impossible to attribute cause and effect to anything around that time.

Ellis drowned. (Sib's pubic hair turned white overnight.) Given the state of his family, Phil asked for and was given a desk job at the Pasadena headquarters. Another baby arrived.

He hadn't really understood the depth of Sib's ongoing anger and despair until a day in May 1980 when her beloved principal (and their family friend), Mrs. Wright, called him at work. "Phil, it's Winona," she said. "Winona Wright. I need you at the school. Sib's okay, but you must come over right now."

At Whitman, he parked next to Sib's Camry and headed to the school's rear entrance, when her teacher friend Angela called to him from the back steps of the equipment shed in a rear corner of the playground. He walked over and she stood with a hand on each railing as if to block his entrance.

"What's going on?" he said. "Is Sib in there?"

"I just want to prepare you. It's upsetting."

"Is she okay?"

"She will be."

Inside, Sib was passed out in her slip on a scruffy old sofa. Mrs. Wright was trying to drape her sweater over her chest and shoulders, but it kept slipping off.

Sib was breathing but completely limp. The room reeked of bourbon. There'd been a spill.

In the small space were a wooden desk and coffee table littered with ashtrays and newspapers. A Philco TV sat on the desk. Sib's dress with the large pink flowers was sprawled on the floor. "What is this place?" he said.

"Apparently it's Pat McCloskey's hidey-hole," said Mrs. Wright. "I knew he had an office back here. But not a drinking den. God knows what's gone on in here."

Phil had met the short, cheerful, barrel-chested janitor at school functions, and he'd long been a recurring character in Sib's nightly monologues: "Pat brought me an aquarium he found, and he'd even fixed the motor. . . . I stupidly left my car lights on but Pat gave me a jump. . . . Guess what Pat brought me? A beautiful old oak desk to replace the cheap Formica-top horror I've had forever." His name came up so often that Eva—who must have been five then—said to Phil, "If you and Mommy weren't married and Pat and his wife weren't married, I bet Mommy and Pat would get married."

"Highly unlikely," Phil had told her.

She'd caught something he'd missed.

Angela gathered Sib's purse and dress, sweater and panties.

He asked how she'd found Sib in Pat's hideout.

"It's our Marie Callender's day. We always drive together,

leave one car here and go for pie and coffee. But I couldn't find her. So I came here."

"But how did you know to look here?"

"We're friends, Phil. Sib tells me stuff."

"But why bring in Mrs. Wright?"

"It was her or the paramedics."

He carried Sib to his Saab, somehow maneuvered her into the back seat. A few blocks from home, she stirred and sat up, then shoved his shoulder. "I love him," she said. "My Patty Pat. And you—" Another, stronger shove. "You can go to hell."

Then she was sick all over the front and back seats.

Phil put her to bed and told the girls, Sally and Eva, that she had a bad flu.

Sib remembered nothing in the morning and, hungover, stayed home.

Mrs. Wright met him at the house that afternoon and held a small intervention. Mrs. W. was very stern. "You will take two weeks off," she told Sib. "You will stop drinking. I know about alcoholics and alcoholism. If you start convulsing or hallucinating, Phil will check you into detox at Las Encinas. At any rate, you will go to the meetings. If you weren't the best teacher I've ever worked with, you'd already be out of a job. But I'm giving you one chance to treat your disease. If you ever drink—if you take so much as a sip—on school property again, you will be fired, and not just from Whitman. I'll make sure you'll never work in the district again."

That scared the hell out of Sib. It scared the hell out of Phil.

He never asked Sib how long it had been going on. He never mentioned the janitor's name to her. (*A janitor!*) He came home early a few days later and found her in the backyard, on the chaise drinking iced coffee and reading a mystery novel. "No booze." She offered him her glass to sniff. He put up a hand—no need.

"So," he said. "Are we done? You and I?"

"Only if you want us to be," she said.

And in that moment, he had the definite sense that a score had been settled. That they were now on even ground. He said, "Let's see how it goes."

When Sib returned to work, a new janitor emptied her waste-baskets.

Sib did stop drinking and went to AA meetings once or twice a week that whole summer. "Not for me," she eventually said. "I hate how they keep trying to cram God down my throat." Her preferred cocktail glass, that green plastic thing, came out again, but she was careful. Hating himself—he knew from Al-Anon that it was wrong—he compulsively checked the level in the bottle of vodka she kept under the sink. A quart usually lasted almost two weeks. If she could keep it to that, he thought, they might manage. And she did keep to it, mostly. Sometimes she'd get a little loose, but only at home.

Can a real alcoholic control their drinking like that? He never really knew.

Maybe because she had cut back, and because Katie—so angry as a teenager—was away at college, or maybe because after six long years, grief had finally loosened its grip, life at home grew calmer. A new, quieter family had formed with just Sally and Eva. No matter how many times Sib batted the girls away—she remained short-tempered and easily annoyed—they kept coming to her, showing her artwork and homework, telling her about their days and their friends, modeling a new hairstyle or cuddling up with her on the sofa. The two made her be the mother they wanted and needed. They beat back her darkness—some of it, at least.

What saved the two of them, him and Sib, unlikely enough, was dominoes. Every night after dinner, epic battles were fought at the kitchen table, with much calling out and laughter. Sally once said that the clack of dominoes was the sound of home.

He found he could talk to Sib as they played; she was so competitive, so intent on beating him, she could hear whatever else he had to say without immediately going on the defensive. When Julia had written asking to meet Eva, he and Sib went back and forth over what role Julia should play in their youngest daughter's life. Sib didn't want her anywhere near the girl, and Phil saw no harm in including Julia in their family—especially since Sib, so caught up in her work, often left the girls on their own. Sib wore him down, quoting endless experts to bolster her arguments that having a second mother around would undermine her authority, and confuse and possibly scar a six-year-old.

He'd continued to send Julia updates and photos, as he had since Eva was born. "That's more than enough," said Sib.

Phil thinks of those last five or six years with Sib, from the early to mid-eighties, as their second good stretch, the first being their family life until Sib went back to school.

With such a chasm of grief in between. And after.

Because that second stretch was also when Sib stopped getting checkups and ignored the lump in her breast. When some part of her had quietly given up.

The sun is beginning to make itself felt, and the mist off the fountain glitters prismatically, and sometimes a breeze sends some spray his way in cooling bursts. He stretches his arms out on the back of the bench and takes a few deep breaths.

He had a dream recently in which he told Sib that he was marrying Yvette. And Sib said, *Does it have to be her?*

He and Yvette were like old familiars who recognized each other on sight, ten thousand miles from home.

From the first, their feelings were in tune: high humored, interested, and sexual. Which couldn't have been more different from what had driven him to Sib. With Sib, he was staking his place in the world, finding a wife to make a home and start a family with. With Yvette, it was more intimate. A nourishment.

They'd made no declarations. They both had children to raise and marriages to tend. Those kids are now adults, the marriages finished.

JP, their son, brought them together.

Last September, when Yvette met him in the Oaxaca airport baggage claim, they both burst out laughing, and she took his hand.

By then they had been talking and writing for six months. He would have flown down earlier, but they wanted to give JP time to adjust. He was angry with Yvette, even as he began accepting Phil. Phil now loves the man—his blurts, his grouchiness, his inability to make his work the least bit comprehensible. His tender devotion to Pilar and their baby. Who knows what JP feels about him; JP's hard to read, but he's kept coming on hikes, initiating most of them. They've probably walked over two hundred miles together, many of them in silence. JP is less enthusiastic about the wedding than Phil's daughters are—then again, enthusiasm is not exactly in JP's toolbox. But he has come to Oaxaca and is at the house with Pilar and little Claudia Jeanne, his brother François and his family, and Yvette's sister, Marie Claire.

Phil's daughters had worried that his feelings were hurt when JP named his firstborn after Claude, but Phil likes to think he had suggested it—or at least preempted any awkwardness.

Back when Pilar was pregnant, Phil had said, "You know, JP, it's a Jewish tradition that babies are named for the recently deceased, which in your case could mean Claude. . . ."

At first, the house in San Felipe del Agua had intimidated him. The street view is a concrete facade half a block long with only a few high, squinting windows and an enormous double door of thick weathered wood and baroque steel straps—a dungeon's door (which in fact came from an old cathedral). The inside is a wonder of light and space, with rooms ranging from vast to intimate. The walls are painted in deep, saturated colors, with railless Barragan stairs running up them like rick-rack to bedrooms and rooftop patios. (No wonder JP worries about his mother and grandmother with those stairs!) Known as the Joubert-Durant House, a husband-and-wife collaboration, it's been featured in *The World of Interiors*, *Architectural Digest*, and *HG*. Yvette still gets work from people who have seen those photo spreads.

The house is comfortable and easy to live in, though it's quite a walk from their bedroom to the kitchen. "Keeps us fit," says Yvette.

At seventy, she is slim and nimble. And tough. She digs in the enormous garden alongside her gardener and hauls heavy bags of groceries from the mercado. She swims laps every day. She has lightness, an ease, and excellent habits. Her closets and drawers are neat, her counters uncluttered and scrubbed, though she makes quite a mess when she cooks. There are no piles anywhere.

The smallest things please her. A good cup of coffee. A tiny green praying mantis, the new bloom on an echeveria. His laugh.

Not much bothers her, except ugly architecture.

The house is lively; she and her mother and Vicky, her mother's seventy-four-year-old caretaker, banter room to room in French, English, and Spanish. In the afternoons, Yvette takes them for a drive, and they stop for a piece of cake or a hot chocolate somewhere. He, too, joins and enjoys these geriatric jaunts.

He will wait until after the wedding to tell his daughters, but he has decided to sell the Altadena house. A young man's dream has become an old man's solitude. If any of his daughters want it, they can arrange something with the others. Otherwise, he'll put it on the market in a month or two.

He and Yvette are planning to build a somewhat smaller, stairless home on a large lot she owns about a mile from where they live now. Higher up, with a fine view of the city and distant hills. The Joubert-Samuelson House. There will be room for many visitors.

They'll fly to California once every season. All their grandchildren are there.

Oaxaca is five thousand feet above sea level and the air is thinner here, the sun more intense. He is dozing a little on the bench. This is one thing that he likes about getting older. Dozing in the sun. All his life, he's seen old men dozing on benches and it never occurred to him that it was a pleasure. Drifting in the shallows of sleep. He doesn't quite dream; it's more a stream of images: intricate patterns of dots, diamonds, leaves, and flowers unfurl like beautiful fabric or wallpaper. Today, there's a parade of faces. Sib's tanned round face, with her brown eyes and cap of coffee-brown hair; Mrs. Wright, her beige hair marcelled in perfect waves, her chin raised, imperious; his mustachioed father is eternally young, as he died in his forties; and his own beloved firstborn son has sticks and pebbles in his curly blond hair, that odd genetic glitch Phil might have thought suspicious except that his own grandfather had that yellow hair. And there's his mother, and his old friend Harry, who was at his first wedding, and it occurs to him then that they are all dead, so perhaps he, too, has died, felled by his heart, or blood flooding his brain.

Shrieks from children playing and a very loud motorcycle wake him up. He blinks to focus. A stray gust sends a wing of water his way from the fountain. Right into his eyes. He wipes it away with his hands.

This is his wedding day. Enough dawdling down memory

lane. He stands and takes a deep breath, and look! Who's coming toward him but Sally and his granddaughters.

"We came out to look for you!" says six-year-old Ida.

"Everyone's waiting on breakfast for you," adds Sibbie, who's eight.

He hugs them, his small, skinny girls, then Sally, who is forty-four, with white in her hair. Walking beside her as the girls skip ahead, he says, "I had a little nap there and the dead were paying me visits until I began to be afraid that I was dead too."

"Oh yes," Sally says. "Dreams and thoughts of death and dying are very common during big life transitions. I mean, think about it: you are in fact leaving one life for another—and your unconscious reads it the same as any death. Anyway, I like to think of all transitions as practice for the big one."

He laughs in a staccato burst. "Is that you or Katie the analyst talking?"

"Am I not allowed an independent idea?" she says. "Actually, I read it somewhere."

He holds her hand and she lets him.

Sibbie and Ida have stopped at the curb at the far end of the park and are making big scooping motions with their arms. "Hurry *up*, you guys," Sibbie calls to them. "People are waiting. People are hungry."

Postscript

Subject: A Question
Date: October 22, 2016

To: Samuelson, Eva
Reply-To: fpoconnor.nyu.math.edu

Dear Dr. Samuelson,

I saw your name in the lineup for the Copenhagen conference, and when I read in your bio that you live in Pasadena, I wondered if by any chance you are related to my fourth-grade teacher, Mrs. Sibyl Samuelson. Mrs. Sam (as we kids called her) was the first person to notice that I was proficient in math and the first person to tell me I had what it took to go to college and beyond—me, the son of a plumber! (I went to Harvard.) She tutored me during her lunch hours, and she also introduced me to the boy who is still my best friend today, who back then was a selective mute,

Sandro Grolio. I owe Mrs. Sam more than I can say. I wish I had told her so when she was alive.

If you are not related, please disregard this note. Either way, I look forward to hearing your paper in Copenhagen.

Yours,
Dr. Fredrick O'Connor
Silver Professor of Mathematics, NYU

Acknowledgments

Bug Hollow owes much to its early readers for their suggestions and encouragement: Lily Tuck, Michele Zack, Victoria Patterson, Kyle McCarthy, Merritt Tierce, and Sue Horton. I am especially indebted to Mona Simpson for her unstinting support, stringent standards, repeated readings, and enduring friendship.

I am grateful, too, to those who generously shared their knowledge and expertise with me, including Kathe Kelly, RN, Dr. Kevin Thomas, Dr. Leah Barlavi, Dr. Benjamin Chu, Dr. Patricia Potter, Kai Bird, Gabe Goldberg, Dorée Huneven, Bernadette Murphy, Angela Gee, Alice Fung, Michael Blatt, and Scott Moyers. Any distortions or factual errors are mine alone.

Joan Weinzettle's exquisite woven art inspired Sally Samuelson's wall hangings.

Many thanks to my agent, Brettne Bloom, for her enthusiasm and advocacy.

I am extremely lucky and grateful to work with the people at Penguin: my editor Ginny Smith, assistant editor Caroline Sydney, publicist Gail Brussell, marketing director Danielle Plafsky, production editor Mike Brown, copy editor Kim Surridge, the book's interior designer Lexi Farabaugh, and cover designer Darren Haggar.

A literature award from the American Academy of Arts and Letters gave me a timely, welcome boost. The Huntington Gardens and Library gave me a quiet place to work.

I also want to acknowledge my creative writing students at UCLA who, week after week, wrote to the prompts I gave them and (sometimes with trembling hands and quavery voices) read their stories aloud in class. Their bravery inspires me. This is a book built on prompts, starting with one I gave my students some years ago: Write a story about a sibling you never had. . .

And finally: Jim Potter's love, humor, intelligence, and excellent Poilâne-style currant rolls fueled the writing of this book.